# Praise for *Unnamable*

"Schrader's supernatural suspense novel boasts skillfully developed characters, relentless pacing, and jaw-dropping plot twists. The writing is filled with profound existential insights…which may remind horror afficionados of the early works of horror master Robert R. McCammon. This novel is horror at its best—dark and deeply, delectably disturbing."

— *Kirkus Reviews*

# Praise for *Bad Realities*

"While Schrader plays around with genres, it's all consistently disconcerting and scary stuff. Characters persistently wind up in harrowing circumstances or, as the title suggests, face some horrible, disturbing truth…the author casts a spell with sharp, concise prose and climaxes that will rattle most readers. Dark, indelible, and gleefully unsettling tales."

— *Kirkus Reviews*

# Praise for *Escaping Midnight*

"★★★★★ Another weird and wonderful collection of compelling short stories. I would certainly suggest that if you have a vivid imagination, you definitely need to read this brilliant book with the lights on."

— *Readers' Favorite*

# ALSO BY ANDREW SCHRADER

*Bad Realities*

*What Goes On in the Walls at Night*

*Vanish Into Midnight*

*Escaping Midnight*

# ANDREW SCHRADER

# UNNAMABLE

BAD PEOPLE PUBLICATIONS

# UNNAMABLE



For information, contact:
Andrew Schrader
http://www.andrewjschrader.com

Bad People Publications
Editing by Karen S. Conlin
Cover photo by Rickey Mizuno & Jordan Harris
Cover design by Jordan Harris
Cover title design by Hannah Nance
Cover model: Brad Geis
Location provided by John Dwyer
ISBN-13: 979-8-9874983-1-6
First Edition: 2024

*The great trees leaned together, the vines ensnared my feet;*
*I heard across the darkness my own heart's thundering beat.*
*Damned be the dark ends of the earth where old horrors live again,*
*And monsters of lost ages lurk to eat the souls of men!*

— "The Dweller in Dark Valley," Robert E. Howard

***

*And a man's enemies shall be those of his own household.*

— Matthew 10:36

***

*The devil takes the hindmost!*

— Children's taunt

# PROLOGUE
## PENNSYLVANIA, 1848

I t happened. The baby was born.

I paced alone in the hallway by the small library on the first floor, the wood creaking angrily with each step. I twisted up my hands, wishing for God to take the thing back, but there was nothing I could do now to convince the Almighty.

After all, I was only fourteen at the time — I, Nathaniel Carter — and what god would listen to me?

The doctor's voice from upstairs reverberated through the ceiling, only to be swallowed up by the shrill screams of the newborn.

I had hoped against hope that the child would abort, that my mother would miscarry. That this . . . sibling of mine would not be allowed to be born.

But my wishes were not part of the plan.

As I walked to the end of the hallway, my glance caught the portrait of the bearded man with beady eyes and a harsh jaw. My father seemed to be glaring at me. I quickly turned to avoid any accusations, wiping the tears from my eyes.

Knock, knock!

I jumped. Christ, my nerves were shot. I went for the front door, my foot snagging on the ragged carpet along the hallway. I stumbled, nearly taking the letter opener on the tiny hallway table with me — the table Father and I had built before he passed. Mother had seemed so touched by the gift, so moved, running her hands through my hair and lightly touching my neck in the way I used to love as a little boy.

But that was all over now.

I opened the door.

"I was on my porch and saw the doctor coming," Angie said, breezing through the doorway and kissing me on the cheek. She wore her usual bell-shaped dress, this one a dark shade of gray with a fitted bodice, complemented by an off-the-shoulder neckline and ruffled short sleeves. "The baby has arrived?"

I nodded in response.

She smiled warmly. "My mother sent me with this." She handed me a large basket filled with fruit, jars of jam, and dried meat. I stared at the contents, struggling to muster a reply or express my gratitude.

"My goodness," she said, unwrapping her scarf and laying it on the rocking chair by the door. "You're sweating." She dabbed at my forehead with a handkerchief.

The cries of the newborn echoed again from upstairs, causing me to flinch. She leaned in and kissed me again, this time on the lips. I returned the kiss mechanically, my mind swirling with dark and terrible thoughts.

"What's wrong, my love? Did the birth go badly?"

I croaked a no.

"Then what is it?"

I opened my mouth to speak, to confess everything that weighed on me, but the words wouldn't come.

How could I explain?

I could hardly admit the truth to myself.

Then —

"Nathaniel!" The doctor's voice rang down, stern and urgent. "Come up here!"

I met Angie's gaze and took her hand. Despair erupted in my guts. I knew what was about to happen. I knew she'd be crushed. *I'd* be crushed.

After all, we'd made so many plans. Our future marriage was but a beginning to a long and fruitful life we had promised to each other. We were young, but our lives were set.

How could I tell her it would never happen?

With a forced smile, I squeezed her hand a little tighter, and together we walked down the hallway to the stairs.

I paused to let Angie pass, hugging the table that held the letter opener. Subtly, I adjusted the cloth runner.

She didn't notice a thing.

Inside the dimly lit bedroom on the second floor, candlelight flickered softly beside my mother, who lay pale and worn on the bed. The exertions of childbirth had left deep marks of fatigue on her face. At the foot of the bed, Doctor Leclaire held the newborn by the ankles, gently smacking its back to clear the mucus from its throat. With careful hands, he then cut the umbilical cord, wrapped the baby in a soft wool blanket, and placed it in its crib, introducing it to its new world.

"Lilith." He approached my mother, placing his hands on her shoulders with a gentle firmness, coaxing her to lie back. "You need to rest."

My mother looked up at him, her expression wan and ghostly. Despite her advanced age for childbirth, she had muscled through. As she always did. "Nonsense," she rasped, pulling herself up into a sitting position despite the blood-soaked sheets around her thighs. Her voice was a dried tobacco rattle.

I stood just out of the candlelight, feeling like a shadow, shapeless and meek.

"You." Mother's voice soured as she noticed Angie in the doorway beside me.

"I was just leaving, Mrs. Carter," Angie said quickly, her voice uneasy. "Congratulations on the birth."

Mother said nothing.

I nodded reassuringly to Angie. It's okay, I tried to convey. I'll be okay.

She gave me a supportive look and retreated down the stairs. I couldn't shake the feeling that my salvation was leaving.

Below, the door slammed.

"Say hello to your brother," Mother said to me. "His name is Jacob."

My feet felt like lead, impossible to lift. Somehow, I managed.

Doctor Leclaire, who had moved aside, was busy cleaning his fat fingers, stained with gore and secreta and excrement. The sight was gruesome — how could so much blood come from one person?

How was this thing called Mother still alive?

My heart pounded furiously against my ribs. Closing my eyes, I drew in a deep, steadying breath before I forced myself toward the cradle, my hands clutching its edges for support.

I opened my eyes slowly and looked inside.

Time froze.

The hideous thing laid in its crib.

A sharp intake of breath choked in my throat. "God, forgive me."

My mother's voice rose sharply. "Look at you. Embarrassed by your own kin. You ought to be ashamed."

I turned towards Doctor Leclaire. "Sir . . ."

But the French doctor clamped a hand on the back of my neck and pulled me closer. I smelled blood and shit on him. "He is a child of God," he said. "You will love him as such. Your brother is simply deformed. There is nothing wrong with that."

"It's not that, it's —" Terror galloped through me. How could I tell him of the abominable thing? I wanted to explain it all — why I could never accept this boy as my brother — but the words eluded me.

Doctor Leclaire's expression hardened as he wagged a slimy finger in my face. "Listen here, you ungrateful whelp. Your father is dead. You are the man of the house now." He tightened his grip on my neck. "You must act like it."

Mother's mouth curved into a smirk. My heart sank.

I heeled backward toward the crib as Doctor Leclaire released his hand. Collecting myself, I faced the imposing figures before me.

"You're right," I said, my voice wavering. "I — apologize."

"Good boy," he responded, his tone patronizing.

"I'll love him as my own . . . and he'll die by my hand."

I yanked the letter opener from my waistband. Raised it high, my intent clear. I aimed for the child's heart.

But the fat man was surprisingly quick.

Bellowing, he lunged forward and slapped my wrist hard, knocking my aim off course. The blade sank into the wooden side of the crib. His powerful backhand took me down; my nose cracked against the impact, blood spraying the wall like gruesome artwork. As he stumbled from his forceful swing, he collapsed on top of me. The back of my head slammed into the wooden floor. Stars exploded in my vision.

Gasping for air, he rolled over and pinned my arms. In a desperate move, I drove my knee up into his groin.

His eyes bulged, his brain registering the impact before he felt the pain. Then his body went limp and toppled over, his mouth in an O shape like some newspaper cartoon.

I took my chance. I scrambled to my feet, each step unsteady as the room tilted around me. I stumbled, caught myself, and made for the door.

Escape was my only option. I knew it then. I'm still convinced of it today. That I would be tried for attempted murder was a certainty. Mother would never help me, not after revealing her true self to me during that past year.

When I learned how evil a mother could truly be.

I shook my thoughts away and kept moving. Snatching my hat and jacket from the hooks in the entryway, I burst through the door and sprinted into the night.

"Nathaniel!" Angie's voice halted me in the tall grass outside the house, right before the wrought iron archway leading to the dirt road. I could tell by Doctor Leclaire's furious shouts that he had recovered. It was only a matter of time before our neighbors woke up. I hooked Angie by the arm and pressed on.

We went until our lungs burned. Well past the "Ironwood: Population Growing!" sign, we finally collapsed onto a fallen tree, both of us gasping for air.

She grabbed my arm and begged me to tell her what had happened.

I gazed at her in dismay.

How could I tell her I'd just tried to kill my brother?

"Just know I had my reasons for what I did," I said. "Believe me. Whatever they say, you have to believe me."

She gazed at me — *into* me. She found something there. Something true. After a moment, her expression softened. "I believe you," she whispered.

I told her I had to go. Any moment now, the doctor would be gathering a mob. They'd come for me.

"Where? For how long?"

I couldn't say. I had no way of knowing. All I could do was embrace her, blocking out everything else for a few precious seconds while I crushed my face into her lavender-scented hair.

A dog barked somewhere in the direction of the road. Voices carried on the wind — men shouting, approaching fast. Closing in. I had minutes left, at most.

"We were going to be married," she said to no one. Her voice was lilting and beautiful. It died on the breeze.

The dog barked again, more urgently now. My heart raced; I felt the raw edge of panic. I kissed Angie deeply, noting every detail — the softness of her lips, the sprinkle of freckles across her button nose. With one last desperate look, I memorized her silhouette against the dim light.

Then, tearing myself away, I ran. Brambles from a dead tree clawed and tore my face as I pushed through. Glancing back, I saw her shape fading into the darkness, merging with the shadows until she was no more than a part of the night herself. I turned and plunged onward.

And I ran . . .

From a failed murder attempt. From my devil of a mother. I ran until I could go no farther. Until I was beyond exhaustion.

My desperate escape landed me in New York, where survival meant picking pockets and living like a rat in the sewers. Eventually, the law caught up with me, and my punishment was conscription into the Army. There, I was assigned to the 4th Kentucky Cavalry and rose through the ranks to captain, forging a team, losing my sense of self, then rediscovering it in the chaos of war.

When you run from something, I've come to realize, you never really make choices in your own life. You delude yourself into *believing* that you are. But all you're doing is trying to stay sane.

I know the truth now. I couldn't have known then.

So I ran.

Yes, I did.

For eighteen years.

# CHAPTER 1
## 1866

Firelight is deceptive. It illuminates, warms, provides comfort, but just beyond where it fades into darkness lies another world.

It's a world I know well.

I wondered if, somewhere in my enemy's mind, they had a preternatural instinct that they were being watched that night. Were they ignoring some internal alarm? Had they been less drunk, would they have known they were about to be attacked?

Four soldiers and I, each armed with rifles, pistols, and knives, were strategically positioned around the campsite, out of the firelight's reach, close enough to see every detail. We had been lying in wait for over an hour, forming a silent perimeter around almost ten men who were reveling in the spoils of their recent looting.

The time for our attack was coming, but not yet.

There were things to do first.

An employer had recently asked me why every Southern guerrilla group still acted as if the war was on. I told him because for them, it was. This particular group of partisan rangers wasn't too bright, I guessed, but not too dumb either, considering they'd ransacked half a dozen towns across Virginia and West Virginia, and even pushed into Pennsylvania. Earlier that day, they'd hit Charlesville just seven miles north, and their spirits were unusually high.

Among them, Creed Sides, the one-eyed man we were sent to capture, showed an unsettling interest in a young girl, barely eleven, shackled and visibly terrified, by the fire.

He plopped down beside her. I gripped my rifle and edged in closer to the bush. I could have shot him dead to rights. But I didn't. I had to wait.

"Have a swig." He held up a mug of something hot. "It'll warm ya up." She stared at the ground to avoid seeing his eye running all over her. He adjusted his eyepatch, leaned in closer, and took a deep inhale. "Ya smell so much like my sister," he said. "How I miss her so." A misshapen and badly scarred hand touched her leg.

That moment almost broke me.

Still, I waited.

I gazed past them, to the opposite side of the clearing, across the fire. One of their men in an open shirt was standing in the brush, only half on guard, his rifle leaning against a tree beside him. He was supposed to be on patrol, but he had a swagger about him that suggested idle drunkenness.

I didn't even see Lieutenant Fowler come up behind him. Just a flash of silver light, the fire catching the blade. The sentry was yanked back. The blade found his voice box quickly. There was no sound.

The enemy's horses, tied to the low-hanging branches of an oak tree farther to the right, knew something was amiss. Animals always do. They screamed hot breath, but the soldiers took no notice. The whinny did, however, catch the little girl's attention, which, in turn, caught Creed's.

"Don't worry about the noise, my turtle dove. I'll take care of ya." Leaning in, he ran his hand up her leg. I'm sure she could almost taste his rotten breath. She shrank from him reflexively.

"Disgusted by me, eh?" A deranged grin appeared. "'Ere's more where that came from."

He stood, beginning to pull down his pants.

Then the girl, that brave little girl, snatched a cup of steaming coffee that had been heating next to the coals and threw its contents onto his crotch. He howled. She turned and crawled in my direction.

That was it. I could wait no more.

I stepped out, training my pistol on Creed, when I felt the rifle butt nearly split my head open. Pure luck, I suppose, that the second guerrilla who had snuck up on me had chosen to butt me instead of shoot. I should have been dead. The force of the blow spun me around, and as I tried to right myself, Creed reared up with a knife that seemed the size of my arm.

I raised my pistol and fired.

His head blew apart like a melon.

I whirled to confront the attacker when three sharp pistol shots rang out. My assailant was hurled backward into the brush. A red mist exploded from his chest. Suspended by the dense foliage, he appeared to float in midair. Then, with a snap of branches, he collapsed lifelessly to the ground.

The rest of the shots came quickly, almost on top of each other. I knew that no bullets were wasted, no unnecessary shots taken. The remaining villains were efficiently dispatched.

That was the measure of my crew.

As I blinked the stars away from my vision, I heard them give the all-clear.

Sergeant Bud Hawkins, who had shot my attacker, holstered his pistol and slung an arm around me. I was still dizzy and needed support. Slowly, my head stopped swimming, and I patted Bud on the back, telling him to finish securing the camp with the others.

I kicked at Creed's boot. Good riddance. He lay at an odd angle, his arms and legs splayed, his head hanging loosely at forty-five degrees. Stuck in the spatter were bits of white teeth and pale gray brain; they led in a trail to the small figure now trembling in the bushes.

"Come on out," I said. "I won't hurt you."

Tiny, olive-colored eyes glinted between strands of dirty blond hair. The eyes didn't seem to register me. The mouth was grim. I understood. I retrieved a horse blanket from one of the dead guerrilla's saddles and covered up the faceless soldier previously answering to Creed. Then I dragged his body aside; we'd need to haul the body with us tomorrow as proof of his death.

I coaxed the little girl from the bushes, sat her down, unshackled her, and started making some hot chocolate. Bud returned not long after with the girl's parents, whom we'd placed a quarter mile down the road before the incursion. When they left, I rekindled the dying fire.

I was plagued by a rotten headache. Splashing some warm water on my face helped, but I knew it wouldn't relieve the pain completely. I also knew there wasn't much I could do for my aching knee or the nerve damage in my arm. I was resigned to the discomfort. But that's what comes with command of an ex-Army unit, a private band of trackers whose primary job is to hunt Confederate leftovers, guerrillas who made it their business to pillage every town they could in the name of the South.

Lieutenant William Fowler approached, wearing his distinctive head wrap adorned with a hawk feather. His nose was prominent, and his eyes appeared deep-set against the puffy scars under them. A half-breed, white and Creek, the contrast of his native wrap and waistcoat at first seemed odd to all who met him. A fine man.

"Tracks lead in one way, sir. Stationed here three days. Made good use of this hideout."

"Any sign of others?" I asked.

"No. I think we're alone now."

"Let's set tripwires on either side, just to be safe. We'll bed down here for the night."

He grunted affirmatively and disappeared into the shadows.

Nearby, a horse whinnied. Bud was rummaging through a dead soldier's saddle. I watched him freeze as he pulled out a bottle of something dark. Whiskey. He stared at it, swallowed dryly. His pockmarked, scarred face made him look older than his late forties. He sported a dark jacket, single-breasted, and a white shirt with a high collar, paired with a brown tie. His expression always had a touch of bewilderment, like a child surprised to be called upon in class. Which I found amusing, because the man used to be — and still played, in our unit — a doctor.

"Bud! Plot out our course for the morning," I said. "I want us up at first light."

He nodded, slowly putting the whiskey away. His hands were shaking, but I wouldn't say a damn thing. He'd only been off the sauce a day or so this time, his twenty-ninth or eighty-sixth attempt at sobriety in the past year. Who could keep count? In any case, no need to embarrass an afflicted man trying to better himself.

A new voice caught my attention. "Bigger fire then, sir?"

Private Rivers, in his impeccably tailored uniform: a dark blue wool coat with polished brass buttons and a slightly curved forage cap. His eyeglasses were spotless, even after a firefight. In his nine months with us, I'd often wondered why someone who could have enjoyed a simpler, easier life in Maine, chose this. He came from a long line of some of the wealthiest shipping merchants in the Northeast. The man was studious, too, and always carried a book or journal with him. An exemplary soldier.

"Yes, thank you," I replied. "And tell McGinley to keep it down tonight."

I glanced at Corporal Lorelei McGinley, the final member of our crew, who was wrist-deep in a dead man's saddlebag. Her dark hair was slicked back under a wide-brimmed hat. She chuckled to herself, pulling out a pack of nudie cards and flashing one in my direction. Winking at me, she pocketed the deck, lit a marijuana cigarette, and moved off to pillage some other dead man's belongings.

During the war, she and her husband had journeyed south to fight with the Union, from Wisconsin to Kansas and then Central Missouri, Lorelei under the name Samuel Grimes. After the Siege of Lexington, when the secessionist state guard had retreated and as the Union made moves on Milford, her husband fell to a sniper's bullet. Tales of her prowess and cunning at pool and poker are still whispered in hushed tones in the corners of bars.

I reflect now how we were all half-breeds, caught in the throes of one victory yet still battling others as the world around us split. We teetered between a dead past and a future charged with the promise of photographs and steam engines. An interregnum where the old world gasped its last breath, while the new one struggled to be born. The pain of slavery was raw, Darwin's tales of evolutionary flux captivated the imagination, and Jules Verne's fantasies of lunar voyages seemed within our imminent reach.

The crackling sap, the soft whistle of burning oxygen from the flames. . . .

Staring into the embers, I drifted deeper within myself. The chirping crickets, the hooting owls, a distant wolf's cry — all merged to create . . . something.

There, just beyond the firelight, where I've always imagined ancient beasts laughing in the dark, she appeared — hazy, with blank, wide eyes and a face prematurely lined and withered, rocking back and forth in her creaking maple chair.

I once believed that as long as I stayed within the yellow glow of the fire, I was safe — that Mother could not reach me. But I've come to realize a deeper truth: no matter how far we propel ourselves forward with trains, steamships, or rockets, and no matter our distractions — work, drink, play — we will never conquer the elemental forces of nature nor escape the nameless horrors within ourselves. We can only hold the darkness at bay for so long.

Believe me.
I'm the one who knows.

25

# CHAPTER 2

ud's voice cut through the morning haze, snapping me out of my lethargy.

The evening had brought no peace, only a series of disturbing nightmares. I'd woken up halfway out of my tent, pajama bottoms twisted around my waist, a cold sweat clinging to my skin, my mother's voice fading from my dreams. In my awkward state, I wasn't sure I'd heard Bud correctly.

"Ironwood, sir." Bud was already busy dismantling his tent.

"We're taking Creed's body to Ironwood, *Pennsylvania?*"

"That's right, sir. It's only half a day's ride. We'll be there in no time," he replied, mistaking my shock for confusion.

Normally, Bud handled our logistical arrangements without any input from me. I rarely questioned our employers' identities or their motives until we collected our dues. Our assignments came from varied sources — here, there, it hardly mattered to me. Staying occupied was all I cared about.

But Ironwood — that was a different story. How could I have missed that detail? I frowned. I never would have agreed to the assignment if I'd known I'd have to deliver Creed's body to the one place I'd sworn never to return.

Old dread stirred in my stomach. It was absurd to be scared after so many years. But fear isn't always rational.

"I reckon I might stay behind."

"Sir?" Bud looked confused.

"You can handle the body. It's just a drop-off. I might take some time here, do some fishing."

"But you're expected, sir."

"Expected? By whom?"

"Our employer. He has another job for us. A big offer, at least that's the sense I get."

I rubbed the stubble on my chin.

"Said he only wants to speak to you," he added. "Name's E. Hoffman Price, ever hear of him? Big industrialist, deep pockets."

With that, Bud returned to his task, unfazed by our exchange. Why would he be? After all, I'd never shared my hometown with him — or anyone else for that matter.

I went about breaking down my tent and the rest of our gear, preparing our horses, and loading my bag. I gave my soldiers their orders, and bathed myself, and gave no sense that anything was out of the ordinary.

But unease gnawed at me all morning as memories of Ironwood flooded back. I'd heard little about the place since I'd left — only scraps of news from passersby like Corporal Jasper McCallan, who'd informed me of my mother's death five years ago. I hadn't pressed for information then and I didn't need it now. Knowing she was gone was enough.

So why this terrible feeling?

I knew, of course.

The knot in my chest tightened at the thought of possibly seeing *him* again.

What was Jacob doing now? Was he even alive? Was he still in Ironwood? Would I recognize him, with his . . . deformities? The thought soured my insides. Hell, I consoled myself, he probably doesn't even know he has a brother.

As for E. Hoffman Price, the industrial titan who had hired us, of course I'd heard of him. Who hadn't? His name was known far and wide as that of the richest manufacturer in the state — a lord among peasants. Why he wanted Creed Sides dead was unclear, and what he desired from us next was another puzzle.

I had to admit, I was curious. And desperate for more work.

I wasn't the only one; the crew was itching for action, for something that paid more than just scraps. Jobs had been scarcer than hens' teeth since the war ended. Every day on the trail we heard more and more stories of broke troops gone reckless and feral. I knew the feeling well.

So I kept my mouth shut. I draped Creed's body with a horse blanket, hoisted him cross-saddle, and broke camp.

As we trekked on, McGinley kept spirits light with her jokes, puffing on her marijuana cigarette. Fowler listened with a silent amusement, in contrast to Bud who seemed distant, his gaze often fixed on the saddlebag hiding the whiskey bottle, his hands shaking slightly. Private Rivers, meanwhile, took to his book while we moseyed along.

Despite their mirth, my heart remained heavy.

Still, I said nothing.


Miles before we reached Ironwood, I could tell it had grown prosperous during my time away. The roads had been widened and macadamized, with limestone shoulders cleanly separating them from the neatly dug ditches. The ornate town sign, adorned with precision-carved flowers spiraling heavenward, announced "Welcome to Ironwood, Pop. 12,000."

As we turned onto Main Street, I tugged my hat down further and tightened my jacket. The road boasted a sturdy mix of bars, stables, hotels, and haberdasheries. Years ago, it had been nothing but a dusty track flanked by shanties. A steady stream of families wove through the streets, the children playing slap-happy hide and seek. Despite the ravages of war and the lawlessness that was following, Ironwood had not just survived; it had flourished.

Crossing Riverton Road, I couldn't help but glance right towards the street where I once lived. Maple and oak trees, matured and lush, veiled most of the homes from view. A part of me wondered about the current state of my old house, barely a quarter mile away.

And if *he* might still be living in it.

I tugged my hat lower.

We stopped the horses just past the intersection at an inn with a large red cedar-planked deck and swinging saloon doors. The building, three stories high and adorned with decadent curlicue trims, was named Headhunter's. Before I could dismount to arrange accommodations for the night, McGinley burst inside, drawn by the sound of billiards, and hollered for a double shot of bourbon. Fowler and Private Rivers made straight for the card tables. Bud lingered at the entrance, collecting his thoughts before stepping inside.

When I got the team settled, I secured Creed's body to my horse once more and set off to meet our employer. Ten minutes up the road, I arrived at a wrought iron gate. I was greeted by two guards carrying Sharps and wearing strange cocked hats adorned with ostrich feathers. More puzzling still, they wore three-piece suits, complete with double-breasted coats and turned-down collars. I had the uncanny feeling of stepping back in time. These were the clothes of my grandparents. They waved me through the gate with stiff, mechanical gestures.

Torches mounted along the driveway bathed the area in a warm, flickering light, brightening an extravagant topiary garden, skillfully shaped from boxwood shrubs. Dueling limestone lions snarled at each other from either side of the path, surrounded by other sculptures: an eagle with outstretched wings, a rearing horse, and a menagerie of smaller animals frolicking at knee height.

What to say about the house itself? You can conjure up an idea.

In the back, three guest houses, each a miniature replica of the main residence, nestled comfortably among the trees, their white columns and sprawling porches mirroring the grandeur of the main house. I suddenly felt the dirt on my cuffs.

Before I could dismount, four men in matching outfits and tricorn hats emerged. Three quickly relieved me of Creed's body, carrying it out of sight. The fourth, a butler in white gloves, gestured toward the mansion. I dusted off my clothes in a futile attempt to appear presentable, then dismounted and followed him inside.

Gilded chandeliers dangled high above me, their crystals casting prismatic light across the polished marble floors. On each side, grand staircases swept the room upward in a graceful symphony of architecture, their railings wrought in sophisticated patterns of iron and gold. The stairs were carpeted with plush, deep red runners, edged with golden tassels. Paintings in silver frames, each the size of a man, likely portraits of the estate's ancestors, gazed down upon me, their eyes accusing me, as if to say: *You don't belong here.*

I was led into the drawing room. I felt as though I were digesting a rich meal. The ceiling there boasted elaborate plasterwork and delicate cornices. Heavy drapes of luxurious velvet in deep burgundy framed the tall windows. A grand fireplace dominated one wall, its mantel carved from local stone and embellished with various artifacts and what I assumed were family heirlooms. Worst of all, two dozen animal heads — lions, tigers, crocodiles, a massive bear — were mounted on the walls, their expressions captured as crude leers. Each one, in its frozen state, seemed to fix its gaze directly upon me.

"Nature is best when she's tamed by man, don't you think?"

An elephantine man with bushy white hair and a three-piece suit lumbered in, leaning on an ivory cane. E. Hoffman Price was a few inches over six feet, about my height. His face, holding a constant sneer, was dotted with soft red stubble at the chin. His weight burdened him; he wheezed from the simple effort of entering. He stepped forward and extended a moist hand.

"Humans in the corner with a whip and chair, is that the idea?" I said.

"Something like that." He gestured for me to sit and walked to a nearby tray of liquor. "I hope your trip was uneventful." He poured us both a stiff Scotch, three fingers' worth, before sitting across the table, exhaling loudly.

I took a sip. I'll give him credit for his taste. Good stuff.

He passed me a heavy satchel. Payment for Creed's body. "You're a tough man to find," he said as I counted the gold coins. "I looked for you for two months before locating your lieutenant. Tell me, is it hard to advertise your services?"

"Advertise?"

"If people don't know you exist, how do you find work?"

I shrugged. "We make do. It helps to stay inconspicuous. Makes it less likely to attract unwanted attention, especially from Confederates holding grudges. We've made our share of enemies." I pocketed the satchel.

"A fair point," he conceded. "In times like these, who hasn't?"

I sipped from my glass, wincing slightly at the sharp, fiery sensation in my throat before it eased into a gentle numbness.

"I sought you out, Captain, precisely *because* you're not easy to find. You don't advertise because you don't need to. People find *you*. Discretion, silence, humility, these are all traits I need right now. I need them very badly, in fact."

He turned to a series of rolled-up papers on the table, unfurled one, and set a few heavy weights on the corners to stop it from curling up.

I craned my neck over the map of Appalachia.

"The war has decimated the currencies of this country," he said. "Doing business in these times has not been for the faint of heart. Treasuries, Confederate notes — the money of man is plentiful and cheap. And worthless.

"The South learned this lesson too late. They racked up debts, took out preposterous loans, and inflated themselves away."

He pointed to a circled section on the eastern part of the map. "There is a mine here. A gold mine. *My* gold mine. The word was it had one of the richest deposits this side of the Mississippi."

"Gold? In the Black Mountains?"

"Yes. A long-held secret. Discovered by the natives, rediscovered by the Spanish, sold to God-knows-who many times over hundreds of years, until it was sold to me." He cleared his throat and drained his glass of Scotch before continuing. "A couple years back, I heard a rumor that the Confederate guerrillas were trying to secure gold to help fund themselves and win the war. I grew concerned."

"You thought they would try to take the mine?"

"It was possible, yes. To be safe, I sent a group to guard the outpost while the miners began excavation. In case any guerrillas arrived, we would be ready."

I struggled to put all this together. It must have shown on my face, for he leaned forward and answered my unasked question. "The soldiers I sent left over a year ago. I've not heard from them. With the war over, it's time we brought them home, wouldn't you say? If they're still there, of course . . .

"The mine is buried deep in the wilderness. A harsh landscape. High altitude. No roads. Avalanches are common. It's isolated as one can get, and still get *to*.

"I need a team to travel to the mine and assess the situation. My property may have been overtaken by Confederates. Perhaps the men I sent are still alive, but there's no way to know. If the mine *has* been compromised, and forces are overwhelming, I will need to know so I can make arrangements. If you can handle the situation yourself, so much the better.

"I would prefer to come with you; I'm no stranger to danger, after all. However . . ."

He knocked his cane against his trouser leg. It thunked against his wooden prosthetic beneath.

"You said you wanted someone who understands discretion," I said. "Why the secrecy?"

"Ah." He circled the table, wincing a bit at the pain from some misstep in his leg. His weight shifting as he sat, he burped, drew a handkerchief, and blotted the sweat from his forehead. "I've taken great steps to ensure *nobody* knows about it, other than those who *need* to know about it. There is more gold in those hills than in the vaults of some governments. It is not inconceivable that the Confederacy, should they find it, would try to fund some new offensive. There is more at stake here than an old man's buried treasure."

"Who did you send before?" I asked. "Soldiers?"

"Yes, ex-Union, a few militia members, a medic of course, a cook, and another fellow . . ." His brow furrowed as he struggled to remember the details. "He had a — what do you call it, a misshapen —" He made a circle with his hand around his face, signaling the area.

My curiosity was piqued. I leaned forward, when —

We were interrupted by a knock. A butler entered and whispered something into his ear.

After a moment, Price nodded, dismissing the man with a wave.

"Apologies for the rushed visit, but duty calls. I've prepared a file; I'll have the details to you early tomorrow morning." He removed a pouch from his drawer and slid it over. "This will be half your compensation." The contents of the pouch spilled across the table. "You'll receive the other half upon your return. For a few weeks' work, I think you'll find it more than acceptable."

I believe my eyebrows rose on their own accord. That amount of gold can make men gasp.

He rose, grunting as he pushed on the cane. "One other thing. Since I can't accompany you, I'm sending four of my men in my stead. Between your two teams, there is nothing you can't handle. You will retain your command, but they will act as my eyes and ears. Trust, as you know, is a rare commodity these days."

There it was — the catch.

"You leave tomorrow."

He exited before I could reply. Left alone, I sat there, the weight of his words settling like dust in the quiet room.

My gaze drifted to the purse of gold coins. In my hand, it felt heavier than before, laden with more than just weight — burdened with a decision. I didn't realize then that choosing to accept this mission would change the trajectory of my life.

And perhaps even the course of humankind.

# CHAPTER 3

My compatriots were snoring like beasts. I was awake — and bored to death. In a nod to our current monetary deficit, I had split the team between only two rooms. Across from me, McGinley sprawled on her twin bed, clad in her filthy long johns. I was almost certain she had her earnings from the card and pool tables stashed in her boots, which she had propped against the wall behind her pillow. She slept soundly. Fowler was in a rocking chair by the window. He had a peculiar habit of sleeping while sitting up whenever he got the chance.

Bud and Private Rivers were in the adjoining room. So far, I'd only heard Bud cry out once that night. Someone needed to keep an eye on him. Though I was restless and wouldn't have minded the distraction, it was Rivers's turn, and I let him take it.

My mind galloped. Something bothered me, only I didn't know what, exactly. Something Price had said? I wasn't sure. I had the feeling not unlike one has when they've forgotten something rather important. It is on the tip of the tongue — only, you can't figure out what it is!

Perhaps it was nothing. I knew too well that when I slowed down, when my brain had a chance to engage with everyday living, my troubles surfaced. So I made it a habit to keep busy — riding, chopping wood, frequenting brothels — anything to exhaust myself and stop my mind from turning inward.

But that night I was without defense. I found myself fixating. What was Price trying to say? Something about "misshapen" before he was interrupted. He was miming around his head, as if trying to say the soldier's head was

—

A snore, loud enough to rip the molding from the walls, erupted from McGinley. The room nearly vibrated. Trying to sleep, or think, through such a buzz saw was pointless.

I checked my pocket watch: 1:35 a.m.


"Bourbon." At the bar downstairs, I plopped onto a stool and rubbed the weariness from my face. The place reeked of stale alcohol and was nearly deserted, save for a few shadows hunched over in their respective corners.

A small, feminine hand — so out of place amidst this grunge — appeared before me, placing a drink on the counter. I smelled something oddly familiar — a perfume of lavender and peppermint. As the hand of the bartender pulled back, my eyes followed it up to the face of the bartender.

It was Angie.

Years had sculpted her more fully, etching maturity into her features without dimming her beauty. Her dark blonde hair, parted neatly down the middle, was pulled back into a tidy bun, showcasing the blue eyes I remembered so vividly.

Caught off guard, I stared a bit too long. She noticed, her glance flitting to meet mine with a flicker of wariness — another nameless patron in her nightly sea of drunks. I was a stranger here, in a place that was once home.

She wiped down the bar, her eyes on her work. "Carnival's in town. Freak show's with 'em this time. Bearded lady, Siamese twins, skeleton man, and all the rest. Why don't you throw 'em a few coins, stare at 'em all damn day? Me, I don't like to be gawked at."

I couldn't help but smile. Yes, she had grown up.

She gave an exasperated sigh, threw her rag on the bar, and turned to face me for the first time. "Do *I* look like a goddamn circus act to you, you son of a . . ." As she saw me, her mouth kind of froze midswear. Her face twisted as she searched mine.

"Hello, Angie."

She stood like a statue for a good five seconds. Then she shook herself out of a daze, reached under the bar and picked up a shot glass. She poured herself one, and after a moment's hesitation poured one for me as well.

"Cheers." Her voice was shaky and wispy, soft like a long-lost memory.

We clinked glasses.

The silence between us was thick and unyielding as we ambled down Main Street, now brightly illuminated by torchlights that burned all night thanks to Ironwood's benefactor, E. Hoffman Price. We walked several blocks in quiet contemplation, giving ourselves time to adjust to each other's presence.

"You're taller than I remembered," she said, finally breaking the stillness. "Do I look like you imagined?"

"Yes. Exactly so."

"How's that? What image *did* you have of me?"

"You're exactly like you, but more so. If that makes sense," I added.

We continued on.

"Are you married?" I asked.

"I was."

"He passed during the war?"

"Yes."

"Was he good to you?"

"He was shit."

Looking back, the lanterns of Ironwood flickered like distant stars. Beyond the town's glow, only the moonlight, the chirping of crickets, and the occasional croak from nearby frogs filled the air. Realizing we were alone together felt surreal. Nearly two decades had passed, yet it seemed as though the intervening time had paused, resuming only at this very moment. We both understood this, recognized the strange intimacy that still lingered between us. We saw each other perfectly.

We never did talk about why I had left or what she had done after I'd gone. I had questions, years of them, but suddenly, the answers seemed less pressing. She was kind enough not to ask about Jacob. I wouldn't have wanted to explain. She understood this wasn't the time for that. It could wait.

We sat on a fallen tree stump. Her face glowed softly in the light that broke the clouds. She took my hand and rested her head on my shoulder. In that moment, I was no longer a soldier; I was a fourteen-year-old boy again, full of promise, yearning for a future with a woman who would give him a family that loved him. I tried to recall other ambitions I'd had back then, but none came to mind — only the desire to be with her.

Hours passed.

All the while, I tried not to ponder the job ahead. My place was with Angie, here and now. The war had ended a year ago; what was I still fighting for? In this new world, with steam and trains and wires promising a bright future, perhaps it was time for me to look forward as well.

She wrapped her arms around me, burying her face against my chest. We sat that way for a long time. The sun rose. She had fallen asleep sitting up on me, and she had salivated in her sleep. My shirt was wet. I smiled. I could have sat like that for millennia, but it was time to go. Before walking her home, I handed her my share of the gold coins. "Keep these," I said. "When I come back, we'll build our future together."

This time, I told her, it was safe to wait.

# CHAPTER 4

**"** We're headed a hundred and sixty miles south into West Virginia, then west another forty or so. The mountains we're going into are pretty hairy, the tallest in the state. The going will be slow, unsteady. It's earthquake country, too, so be prepared for avalanches.

"We'll circle east near Judy Gap, bypassing Barren's Point" — I tapped the spot on the map — "and approach the mountain's keyhole at its base. That'll be the toughest going; apparently getting wagons up through the keyhole is a real bitch. It's likely we won't return the same way. Instead . . ." I traced a path on the western edge of the roughly sketched mountains. "We'll emerge on this side, then circle back around, heading northeast."

I looked over the faces of both crews, weary already from the heat of the day's travel. My soldiers — Fowler,

Bud, McGinley, and Private Rivers — stood to the left, separated from the new unit, which consisted of the four men provided by E. Hoffman Price.

Their outfits made me wince in secondhand embarrassment. All of them wore matching three-piece suits and double-breasted coats, and three had the same cocked hats decorated with ostrich feathers as Price's servants. The fourth, Mister Reagan, their commanding officer, wore a bowler hat. Between the hat and style of dress, he looked topsy-turvy and out of time. A bushy thing you might call a beard blended with an equally bushy mustache, so thick there seemed to be no mouth separating them. His eyes were beady, black, and buried.

The second in command, Sergeant Darrow, had sharp, deep-set eyes, paired with a thin, tightly drawn mouth. He too, wore a beard, though it was shorter, redder, and patchier. His intense gaze seemed drawn to Sergeant McGinley in particular, which I later learned was due to her having taken him for fifty dollars in a pool game at Headhunter's. The fact that she was the only woman in our group did not escape notice either.

The other two, twins named Clive and Monte, were indistinguishable to me.

Price had introduced these men the morning after my night with Angie. They were former Red Legs, abolitionists who had chased Quantrill during the war.

My own encounters with the Red Legs had left a bitter taste. Near Lawrence, while pursuing a Confederate guerrilla group, my men and I stumbled upon the aftermath of one of their attacks. We'd arrived from the south, ditching our horses some five miles out and advancing the rest on foot. We found the Confederates butchered and scalped, their naked bodies scattered across the lakeshore. From a distance, I watched a Red Leg meticulously lay a body over the rocks, carefully draping the intestines on the stones. Later, we learned that the dead were not enemy soldiers but ordinary civilians — men of age whose only crime had been remaining neutral in the war.

Fighting for the Union didn't make a man honorable. Many Northern families feared the Red Legs more than Confederates, for they would raid Union towns as ruthlessly as enemy ones if they suspected insufficient loyalty.

In war, I'd learned, virtue is rare. Chaos reigns. Anything goes. All things find a justification.

After meeting with Price and the men in front of Headhunter's Inn, we'd loaded onto horses and our wagon the food and munitions that had been delivered. Salted and smoked meats, stacks of hardtack, dried beans and lentils, jars of dried fruits — apples, peaches, and apricots — pickled vegetables and other canned goods. A couple sacks of flour and cornmeal, tins of coffee and tea, a cone of sugar, half a bushel of salt, and a wheel of hard cheese. Fowler requested preserved quail eggs. McGinley's requirements of local marijuana and whiskey were stowed as well.

Then there were our tents, blankets, and cooking utensils. Large water barrels were positioned carefully in the wagon, along with lanterns, oil, matches, ropes and pulleys for navigating terrain, map and compass, horse feed, and other essentials.

Now, half a day's ride from town, we paused for lunch while I outlined the general plan.

Darrow spat a glob of something black and flicked his finger toward the map lying on the rock. "So, we get past the keyhole to the mine, what then?"

"We'll assess the situation," I said. "See what we find and act accordingly."

"*Assess the situation*," he said under his breath, grinning, revealing a wad of chewing tobacco the size of a baby's fist. He turned to Mister Reagan and said softly, "Got ourselves a smartass commander."

A tense silence followed. While they were under my command in terms of strategy, it was clear on this first day that Sergeant Darrow was testing my resolve.

I was about to speak, when something cracked in his face. He jumped about six inches, as McGinley quickly retracted her leather cow whip. The bastard grabbed his nose; the whip honked him good, and boy, did he feel it.

Laughter erupted from the group, including the twins and Mister Reagan. Darrow, embarrassed, regained his composure, and for the moment, any challenge to my authority was quelled.

We made good headway through the mountain valleys, sheltered by pines, maples, and oaks. Wide canopies shielded the forest floor from the sky. By noon, the foliage became so thick it blocked out the sun altogether. Daylight felt illegal. It felt as though we'd crossed into a different realm.

Then, something strange occurred. A few minutes after entering this darker part of the forest, I noticed Fowler steering his horse off the path. I nudged my mount to follow, motioning to the others to go on without us.

He stopped some fifty feet off the trail, his gaze transfixed on what looked like a dandelion. Only, unlike the small, wispy flowers every child has blown, its bloom was the size of a dinner plate, perched atop a stalk as robust as a walking stick.

"Never seen anything like it," he muttered, touching the stalk, before straightening and walking over to examine a new plant.

I climbed off my horse and approached. The bush, about my height, bore teardrop-shaped foliage, each leaf lined with a delicate fringe. Under the day's waning light, they shimmered in a spectrum of blues and purples that seemed alien to the Appalachian wilderness.

Next to it, another plant hosted clusters of flowers, each spiraling inward like a dark labyrinth. Their maroon was so deep it verged on black, and each petal appeared subtly illuminated from within. The aroma they released into the cooling air was an intoxicating mix of sweet and spice. It reminded me of the mountain laurel familiar to these parts, with its evergreen leaves and bunches of blooms. But its foliage had an uncanny iridescence; its blossoms were too intricate, too. This was no mountain laurel I knew. And why did the leaves have such feathery edges?

"The plant both climbs *and* spreads on the forest floor," Fowler said, rubbing his hands in the dirt. "Strange."

"Some invasive species?" I asked, glancing ahead. The crew had already disappeared down the trail, leaving us in an eerie solitude. Shadows grew even thicker. The underbrush remained motionless. Birdsong was absent.

The unnatural quiet, the void of sound, set my nerves on edge.

Fowler never answered. The forest held its breath, and so did we.

Two fires were made, one for us and the other for the second crew. There was an unspoken agreement to keep to ourselves. Frankly, I shared the disinterest in mixing with them. We each claimed our areas, a good thirty-five yards apart, and simply sat by our fires. The camp was quiet, save for the occasional comment and Bud's soft cursing about the chill as he reached toward the flames for warmth.

McGinley produced a bottle from her coat, its contents glowing. She took a swig, her throat working the liquid down before she offered it to the rest of us. I hesitated as it made its way to me, mindful of Bud. My own thirst for a drink had been strong these past days, but something held me back. I declined with a wave of my hand.

"Hell, boss," Bud said. "Don't want you changing your ways because I can't handle myself."

I shook my head. "Fire's warmth is enough for me tonight."

"Well, then," McGinley said, producing a few cigars, "been saving these. Figure tonight's as good a time as any, right?" She lit hers with a twig from the fire, then offered them to Bud, Rivers, and me. She turned to Fowler, tried to give him one, but he was sitting away from us, peering into the brush. He seemed to be on high alert. Hadn't spoken more than a few words since we'd found those strange plants. He was giving me the creeps. I turned back to the fire and tried to enjoy myself.

As the day waned, sleepiness crept in. The crackle of the fire grew dim and distant in my ears. My eyelids grew heavy. Thoughts of Angie — her look, her scent — drifted pleasantly through my mind. Mighty fine, I mused, replaying our reunion over and over. Around me, the others were also succumbing to sleep's gentle pull.

Just as I was on the verge of kicking off my boots, Private Rivers's voice pierced the calm.

"Lieutenant?" He nodded towards the edge of our campfire light, his gaze fixed on something in the brush.

I opened my eyes, following his look to where Fowler was already positioned, crouched and statue-like. After a tense moment, Fowler raised his hand in a subtle signal for us to hold and, with his pistol leading, cautiously stepped into the brush.

Without a word, we all rose slowly. My hand reached for the pistol on my belt. Already loaded. I stayed still for a moment, absorbing the sudden tension in the air, then tiptoed between the leaves, aiming to flank Fowler about fifteen to twenty feet to his right.

Something was out there.

Pushing aside overhanging tree limbs, I strained my eyes, trying to adjust to the patchwork of darkness and moonlight filtering through the leaves. Fowler, only dimly visible, moved with stealth and urgency, already a good ten paces ahead.

Then —

A soft rustling. I paused, held my breath, trying to pinpoint its source. My grip on the pistol tightened. As suddenly as it had begun, the rustling ceased. A pressing silence followed. I waited, listening, but the forest remained still.

I sensed Rivers and McGinley moving cautiously to flank me on each side. Bud, I assumed, had remained at the camp. Whether the second group had noticed our absence, I couldn't be sure.

Struggling against the forest — I had worked myself into a tight spot within the brush — I risked making more noise as I peeled leaves from my face and crept forward. Still, I saw nothing.

A firm hand landed on my shoulder.

I spun around.

But it was only Fowler. Somehow, he had managed to get beside me without making a sound. He held a finger to his lips.

*Stay quiet.*

He pointed his fingers in a V-shape, signaling me to look deeper into the forest.

Moments passed.

Fowler raised his pistol again as —

A crouched figure burst from the bush.

Moonlight glinted off a blade, and I instinctively dodged left. The figure swung his knife wildly, missing and pinwheeling before toppling over.

It was a man, I was sure of it then. He hit the dirt hard, the blade skittering into darkness. Instantly, we were upon him, pinning him to the ground. McGinley, efficient as ever, pulled her restraints from her belt and quickly hogtied the struggling man, who was whimpering incoherently. Despite the darkness, I could see his frailty. His arms were thin as twigs. He offered little resistance.

We dragged him back through the brush, face down, and dumped him into the circle of firelight. Our other campmates sprang into action, quickly securing the area.

After Fowler gave a satisfied nod indicating the area was clear, we focused on the figure at our feet.

A pitiful sight.

The man was skeletal, his skin taut over protruding bones. His shirt was more rag than fabric, barely clinging to his emaciated frame. His feet were bare and battered, with a bloody bone jutting grotesquely from a mangled ankle, crudely bandaged in a poor attempt to stabilize it. Froth had formed around his pale, dry lips, and his eyes were hollow, rattling in their sockets. One ear was torn in half, flapping against his head. He continued to mutter gibberish, seemingly unaware of his surroundings.

The insignia on a ragged piece of cloth over his breast caught my eye — it read "Ironwood Outpost," and below that, his name.

"Seamus. Seamus MacReady."

His roving eyes caught mine, flickering with a faint glimmer of recognition, acknowledging that I was, indeed, human. I recoiled slightly from the foul, gaseous odor emanating from him as he gasped — his gums were rotted and yellowing.

Clearly, this man wasn't hunting us.

He was insane.

"You are Seamus MacReady." I repeated, more gently this time. "If you promise not to fight us, I can untie you. Can you do that?"

He nodded after a tense moment, his eyes shutting tightly as he took a deep breath.

Bud quickly cleared a spot next to the fire. "Bring him here, get him warm!"

We untied him and vigorously rubbed his arms and legs to stimulate circulation. He lay there, limp and shivering, while McGinley handed him a cup of steaming coffee. His eyes bobbed as he grasped it, a blanket now draped around his shoulders.

After giving him a few minutes to settle, I resumed the interrogation. "You came from the outpost at Ironwood?"

Coffee dribbled from his lips as he tried to focus on me.

"What happened there?" I asked. He seemed confused by my question, his gaze lost in the fire. "Were you attacked? Was it Confederates?"

No response.

"Look." Bud pointed at a spot near his stomach. I peeled back the remaining cloth, revealing a nasty, maggot-infested wound, a vicious gash that looked like something had clawed through his flesh like cheese.

"They came . . ." MacReady whispered hoarsely, his voice trailing off as he stared vacantly. "Took them. I tried . . . to stop it. But I couldn't. We . . . were betrayed."

"Who? Who came?"

He didn't answer.

"Look at me. *Tell me what happened.*"

His face twisted as he struggled to remember. "They laid siege . . . long time . . . long time . . ."

Fear stole over him like an eclipsing shadow. He trembled uncontrollably.

Cupping his face, I urged him, "Who was it, Seamus?"

But he was lost, drifting into a hallucinatory memory. His eyes widened in terror as he glanced upward, as if some horribly tall creature stretched in his mind.

"They were not men," he whispered faintly.

A shudder racked his body, and then he convulsed, foam now bubbling from his mouth. Bud snatched a stick to prevent him from biting his tongue, while shouting for morphine. Rivers returned with a needle, and as it sank into Seamus's flesh, his haunted eyes perhaps glimpsed an ancient abyss between the living and the dead, the possible and impossible. The shadows in his mind continued to stretch.

Then the morphine took hold and —

Oblivion.

# CHAPTER 5

Two days passed without incident.

The terrain became rockier and more challenging as we gained elevation, but the rigorous pace helped distract us from the new, unsettling tone of the mission. The arrival of MacReady had cast a tense and somber mood over our group.

On the morning following his disturbing episode, we found that the Irishman, despite the morphine and his restraints, had become so agitated during the night that he had bitten off his own tongue.

After some deliberation, we decided it was inhumane to leave him to wander the wilderness alone, effectively sentencing him to death. Nor could we afford the time to turn around and bring him back to Price right then. We were already days into our journey, and I couldn't spare the men to escort him. Besides, given his connection to the outpost, he might still have information we could use. In the end, we decided to splint his leg and keep him restrained, placing him in the wagon among the supplies, concealed behind a curtain.

The tongue was not found.

What did I think of his "they were not men" remark? Not much, I admit. I figured he was insane. I did think it likelier than before that the fort had been taken over by Confederates; maybe by sheer will he'd escaped after a long imprisonment. I could tell he'd been out in the forest a long time, in either case. And almost anyone, becoming half-starved and exhausted, would go a bit batty.

So I thought little of his warnings.

It was a mistake I would come to regret.


Exhausted from the day's trek, both crews plopped yet again next to our respective fires. Behind us, the wagon groaned under MacReady's shifting weight. I offered to let him out for a bit, but he preferred the confines of his makeshift cell.

Private Rivers, stoking the fire for warmth, voiced the question that had been on everyone's mind for some time.

"Do you believe MacReady, sir? About what he said happened at the fort?"

"Which part?"

Rivers didn't want to say the words. "About who attacked them."

We all knew what he was referring to.

*They were not men.*

McGinley, methodically cleaning her pistol, responded. "He was alone in in those woods for weeks. That's enough to mess up anyone's mind."

Bud turned his attention to Fowler, who had distanced himself from the group and was wrapped tightly in his coat. "Lieutenant, what do you think? You think he's crazy?"

Fowler, ever deliberate, took his time before answering, his gaze fixed on the flickering flames.

Bud pressed on, his tone edging toward accusatory. "You know something, don't you? What is it?"

We waited.

"When I was a boy," Fowler said finally, "we lived among the Creek. My mother's tribe. Father was a fur trader. As a white man, he was not accepted by many in our tribe, so we moved frequently. Never stayed in one place more than a year or two. One winter, close to here by the Black Mountains, we camped out with a few other families, away from any settlements."

He paused. "One night, we were sitting around the fire. Everyone was tense, uneasy. A few days before, a man named Shines Like the Sun had disappeared. I overheard whispers among the elders . . . they talked amongst themselves about the people who lived in the rocks. About how men would sometimes vanish into the night and never return. They never heard any screams. They saw no signs of a struggle. No blood. Nothing.

"Everyone thought Shines Like the Sun was gone forever. But early the next morning, he suddenly reappeared. When he returned, he came back *cananee*. It means crooked. Bent." Shadows and firelight danced off his face. "I was asleep in the tent and was awakened by his scream as he wandered back to camp. My mother told me to stay in the tent, but I disobeyed her and saw Shines Like the Sun. The man was covered in blood. His arms were broken, bent in all the wrong places, and he could barely speak. He claimed he'd been taken by the 'men who were not men' who lived in the rocks."

Private Rivers cut in, incredulous. "Those were his exact words?"

Fowler nodded solemnly. "Yes. And whatever he experienced out there broke him. My father said he never recovered; he went *cananee*, twisted by whatever horrors he saw.

"Just like our new friend here."

He jerked a thumb toward the wagon, when —

We'd been so absorbed in Fowler's story that no one noticed MacReady leaping to the ground with a thud, stirring a cloud of dust into the fire. The flames hissed.

Sergeant McGinley's hand shot to her pistol, but MacReady showed no sign of aggression. He shakily raised a finger, pointing at Fowler. Bud and McGinley were ready to intervene, but Fowler's firm "Wait!" held them back. The half-breed and the crazed man locked eyes. We watched as MacReady, wild-eyed, dropped to his knees, scavenging the ground for a stick.

With frantic energy, he began to scratch in the dirt, first an oval, then a longer shape beneath it.

"What the hell is that?" McGinley muttered, peering over.

The crude sketch resembled a body — a grotesque figure with a snout-like face and a jaw filled with sharp, triangular teeth, more akin to railroad spikes than anything natural. Beady eyes were set deep into the head of what could only be described as a monstrous caricature of a boar.

A hideous thing.

MacReady, catching my eye, pointed urgently at his drawing, then clapped his hands together, mimicking an explosion.

"You fought *this*?" I asked.

He nodded vigorously, his hands twisting together in an agonized dance. He released them slowly, sweeping over the drawing as if to show the scale of the encounter.

"And you won?"

MacReady's face fell. He shook his head.

"You mentioned a betrayal," I pressed. "Someone betrayed you to this creature?"

He nodded.

"Who?"

He turned back to the dirt.

"Hell's he drawing now?" McGinley grumbled, spitting into the fire.

I leaned in as MacReady's hands moved again, not to draw but to write.

The group closed in, the flickering firelight illuminating the words scrawled in the dirt, clear for all to see.

I blinked.

I did not believe.

But there were the words. Clear as day.

# jacob carter

# CHAPTER 6

I blinked again. There must be a mistake. My mind couldn't make sense of it.

In stunned disbelief, I took a step back.

*Jacob Carter.*

The name echoed through my mind. Was I caught in some twisted dream?

It couldn't be real, could it?

My . . . brother?

I stared hard at MacReady, trying to pierce through the madness with my gaze.

"About eighteen years old?" I prodded, needing confirmation.

His response was a giggle through his brown, rotted teeth — a sound that chilled me. Reveling in a private joke at our expense. The air around us thickened with the stench of his filth as he soiled himself by the fire.

Overwhelmed, I stumbled back and hurried to my tent. Inside, my hands trembled as I struck a match and lit a candle, the flicker of light doing little to steady my nerves. I dove for my pack, searching frantically for the dispatches Price had handed me as we left — documents I had neglected in the rush of departure. Now it was imperative I find them.

I fumbled with the leather sleeve, papers scattering in a wild flurry. I snatched them up, holding each one to the candlelight with shaking hands.

Could it really be him?

Price had sent twenty-three men to the mine. Here were the names, ages, small bits of history attached.

*Thaddeus Hargrave. Ezekiel Standish. James Whitlock. David Browning. Barton Bragg.*

I nearly jammed a fist in my mouth.

*Jacob Carter.*

Next to his name, it read, simply: *18 years of age. Ironwood native. Deformities of the head. Commissioned as Private.*

"My God!" The words slipped out as reality began to twist.

It seemed implausible, yet there it was, laid out clearly before me. Ironwood was big, but not like New York or Philadelphia. What were the odds *another* Jacob Carter had been sent to Ironwood Outpost? Not to mention one with noted "deformities of the head"?

The chances were nil.

Had Jacob really betrayed his unit? Who had he aligned himself with?

Was he responsible for whatever horrors may have transpired at the outpost?

"Sir?" Bud called for me from outside the tent.

I let out a sharp breath. "Yes?"

He pulled back the tent flap, his expression cautious as he took in my disheveled appearance. Papers were scattered around me on the ground. He cleared his throat and lowered his voice. "The others are waiting for your orders, sir."

"Right," I said, hastily gathering the papers. "Tell Fowler to set up shifts for the night watch. And if MacReady says anything else, I need to know immediately."

"He may rouse in the middle of the night —"

"Then wake me!" I snapped, more harshly than intended.

Bud nodded, a trace of concern flickering in his eyes. "Understood, sir." He backed out, letting the tent flap fall shut.

Alone again, I drew a deep, unsteady breath. Sleep was out of the question at this point. I grabbed the papers once more and uncorked a bottle of brandy I'd been saving. Every detail mattered now; I needed to understand exactly what we were stepping into.

I settled in for a long night of reading.

# CHAPTER 7

It was like gravity, I decided later. Particles drawn together, not by mass but by significance. That I, having fled my hometown, would be drawn back to my brother was a fate I couldn't escape.

Emerging from my tent the next morning after a night buried in commission documents, I felt the weight of secrecy. The papers held no hint of any link between Jacob and me, and none of my troops had questioned the commonality of our last name, Carter. I had guarded this part of my past for eighteen years, unwilling to unearth questions I couldn't face, questions that could derail our mission.

But I knew the real reason. If I could stuff this knowledge deep inside, I could avoid confronting the ghosts that had haunted me for nearly two decades.

But avoiding them was not to be.

Gravity, see?

We aimed to cover eighteen miles that day, but the rising elevation and increasingly rocky paths, scarred by frequent earthquakes, slowed our progress.

When no one was looking, I reached into my saddlebag for the flask of brandy I'd stashed there, seeking solace in its burn. But even as the liquor hit my throat, the haunting memories surged — staring down at Jacob in his crib, his face more beast than boy, the memories of what had happened before he was born flooding back.

Before —

No.

NO.

I shook my head.

Better thoughts. I must find them.

Angie.

Yes.

I longed to abandon everything — the mission, my crew, Jacob — and escape. Perhaps Angie and I would head south to the swamps, or even west to the towering redwoods of California, where a new America was rumored to be taking root. A place of crisp, clean waters and bustling commerce.

I wanted to believe a new beginning was possible.

I *had* to believe.

As we inched up the mountain, the narrow path barely allowed our wagon to pass. On foot now, with our horses in tow, we followed Fowler's grimly determined lead. In the past hour, we had barely covered three hundred feet.

Glancing fearfully over the cliff's edge, my grip tightened on the reins. Each step was a struggle for stable footing, as gravity seemed eager to pull me hundreds of feet into the dark canyon below. Wiping sweat from my brow, I tried to focus on the path ahead.

According to the map, the keyhole — a natural rock formation leading to a plateau with a small lake — was just a few bends away, no more than five hundred feet. The lake was marked as our camp setup point.

Suddenly, I felt strange.

I began to sway.

Nausea.

Dizziness.

I staggered, nearly losing my balance. I knew I needed to sit, but before I could even bend my knees, the ground vibrated ominously beneath my feet.

Oh, no.

"Earthquake!" someone shouted.

I lurched toward the wall to my right and pressed my back against it, huddling into it for protection. Everyone else followed suit, abandoning their horses and grasping at thin roots protruding from the wall for support.

Boulders careened onto the path. One slammed into the ground just between my horse and Bud's. I grabbed

Bud and yanked him toward the wall. His face was a mask of fear as he clutched his horse's lead, struggling to maintain balance.

I scanned our surroundings quickly. The rest of our group had made it to the wall, spreading out along a hundred-foot stretch. But the wagon, left exposed in the open, was dangerously vulnerable.

I peered up, mouth agape. More boulders tumbled down the mountain toward us. The hand of God Himself must be launching them, I thought.

The avalanche bore down.

A massive boulder crashed and rolled, fracturing the wagon's side, ruining the axles, and pushing it within inches of the cliff's edge. The lead horse whinnied as it slid over the side. It dangled helplessly, the swingletree creaking loudly as the beast hung in its harness.

Clive, the driver, stood, poised to jump for safety, ready to abandon the supplies. But glancing upward, he hesitated.

His skull imploded as a stone more than ten feet wide flattened him with a dull thud, snapping the spine of the second horse and sending the battered wagon teetering over the cliff's edge. Only the rear wheels remained on the precipice.

Time seemed to turn surreal then, for MacReady poked his head out from behind the curtain separating the driver's nest from the wagon's hold. He appeared totally unbothered by the chaos. Yawning, he ducked back behind the curtain just as the wagon plunged over the edge, disappearing into the abyss.

Our supplies followed down the mountain, crashing through treetops and smashing apart on the unseen rocks below. As the earth finally stilled, all was quiet except for the eerie pitter-patter of dirt and pebbles drifting down like ghostly rain upon our heads.

"God's split us asunder." Mister Reagan grasped the cross around his neck, staring blankly into the distance.

After salvaging what little remained of our supplies, I urged everyone to stay close to the rock wall, warning of potential aftershocks and the lack of shelter further up the trail. Sergeant Darrow promptly announced he needed to shit and disappeared from view.

Monte, who'd just lost his brother, sat hunched at the cliff's edge. His gaze was fixed on the canopies below, searching for a sign of the fallen wagon. "He loved those horses," he muttered.

My thoughts turned to the provisions we'd lost: two months' worth of food, barrels of fresh water, jars of pickled fruits and vegetables, dozens of pounds of beans and lentils, ten pounds of coffee, five pounds of tea, a hundred pounds of salted meat, fifty pounds of flour, thirty of cornmeal, our utensils, weapons, and other essential supplies. Not to mention the horses. And beyond the material losses, the absence of the two men who had died now cast a heavy pall over us all.

Bud, McGinley, and Fowler were discussing something in hushed tones. Joining them, we all gazed at the gaping chasm that had torn open on the path behind us. Its sheer size made it clear that our way back was closed. We'd been forced into moving forward into the unknown and uncharted territories that lay ahead, whether we wanted to or not.

There was no abandoning the mission.

There was only one way out.

Through.

# CHAPTER 8

With our lightened load, it took only a couple hours to reach the keyhole at the top of the rocky trail.

The sun, now a deep red, hastened its descent, stretching long shadows across the rugged terrain. A cool breeze nudged us gently from behind, as if pushing us onward past the keyhole and onto the plateau. We planned to camp by the lake just ahead, where we hoped to find food and some measure of comfort.

Under different circumstances, the view of the lake, cradled between northern and southern mountain peaks, would have been breathtaking. The way the sun traced its daily path directly between these peaks, aligning perfectly with the trail that led to our outpost and the mine, did briefly lift our spirits.

But only briefly.

I've given up trying to sleep. I wake up every night now, because of the creeaaaaaking on the floor above me. The warped floorboards, underfoot of the thing upstairs.

Something sour rises in my throat.

I want to run.

So badly, I want to run.

But what good would that do?

I track the creaking noises with my eyes. Catch myself praying to God as if not of my own volition, as if something deeper is trying to force its way through my mouth.

The doorknob turns . . .

I roll onto my side, clutch the covers around my neck. The blankets will protect me from the shadowed figure silhouetted in the dim candlelight creeping into the room.

I squeeze my eyes shut.

I wait.

The room fills with the palpable sensation of being watched, a heavy, invisible presence lingering interminably. The air grows dense and stifling.

Something is here. It is hungry.

I pray for it to change its mind, to turn and go. Almost every night, it comes for me. I never know exactly when, but it comes. Why me? I'm just a boy.

My heart sinks as once more the floorboards groan.

So, it will be the same tonight as always.

The thing will stay.

My testicles recoil into me. My body runs cold.

*It's time.*

*I won't resist.*

*A hand trails over the cool sheet along my back, then draws it away, baring my skin to the room's chill.*

*Don't wake, the voice whispers. I'm not really here.*

The next morning, I called reveille at 0630 but didn't rush the troops. We opted for rest over hunting for fresh food before dawn, knowing we needed more time to repack and strategize.

For a moment, I set aside thoughts of the outpost, Jacob, and the deaths of Clive and MacReady, focusing instead on my troops. McGinley seemed alright, except for a few scrapes and bruises. Fowler, Bud, and Private Rivers appeared unscathed. The others — Monte, Darrow, and Mister Reagan — also seemed fine, though I noticed Darrow wincing and clutching his groin as if nursing a strain.

By midday, I called for volunteers to hunt deer. Monte stepped forward, likely seeking a reprieve from his grief. Private Rivers joined him. After buttoning their greatcoats and packing their rifles, they headed into the eastern forest.

They had been gone about twenty minutes when a gunshot broke the silence. I was scrubbing my socks by the lakeside; the others were splitting wood. Thinking nothing of it, we assumed they might have brought down some game.

Then the scream came.

I stopped, listening intently.

The sun was setting, and the dense trees barred any view into the forest. Where had it come from?

Then a second scream, abruptly silenced.

Then a rifle report. Another.

Another.

Immediately, I dropped my socks and sprinted to my tent to grab my rifle, revolver already at my hip. As I rushed toward the woods, barefoot in my boots, I felt an eerie sense of *déjà vu*. I recognized something in those screams.

Despite my dread, I pushed through the thick brambles and foliage. Glancing back, I saw Lieutenant Fowler and Sergeant McGinley close behind, while Mister Reagan and Sergeant Darrow lagged slightly to the left.

We continued on. Pausing momentarily, our ears strained for any guiding sound. Then, three sharp cracks echoed from somewhere ahead. We plunged back into the underbrush, ducking and dodging, propelled forward by the urgent gunfire. A low branch slashed my cheek as we broke into a clearing.

Private Rivers was wildly firing two pistols into the shadows. I shouted his name, he spun around, panicked, and his pistol discharged. A bullet struck Mister Reagan, who fell with a cry. Then Rivers's pistol clicked empty. Seizing the moment, I tackled him to the ground.

Overcome with raw, unbridled terror, he gnashed his teeth, screaming incoherently. I pinned him, but he fought back with an animalistic fury, scratching and clawing at anything he could reach. His nails raked across my face, stabbing deeper into the fresh wound on my cheek. I managed to land two sharp punches to his face, and he lay still beneath me.

"Where the fuck is Monte?" Darrow shouted, scanning the clearing with his pistol drawn. His voice echoed off the trees.

I looked around. He was nowhere.

Then, my eye caught something across the clearing — a patch of leaves glistening with blood that dripped steadily onto the dirt. My gaze followed the trail. I saw more red.

"Cover Rivers," I ordered McGinley, then darted through the brush after the blood trail, Mister Reagan following despite clutching his bleeding shoulder, gritting his teeth through the pain.

We moved swiftly, the trail leading us to the edge of the dense forest. Abruptly it opened to a prairie, hemmed in by towering boulders standing sentinel. An eerie, almost unnatural light hovered above the clearing, rendering everything still and silent. This place felt untouched, unkind, unwelcoming.

Our soldier — and whoever had taken him — had vanished.

Could they be hiding in the tall prairie grasses, watching, waiting?

With my pistol ready, I edged toward the open prairie when Mister Reagan's firm grip on my bicep halted me.

"Stop. Hear that?"

I strained my ears. Silence. I shook my head; I heard nothing.

Mister Reagan swallowed hard, his forehead beading with sweat. "Exactly."

I watched the clearing. He was right. No noises.

It was much too quiet.

His grip tightened painfully. "They want us to go out there. They want us exposed."

Who were they, and why did they take Monte?

As if he read my thoughts, Reagan murmured, "They want him for something. *They want us all.*"

I looked again. Something *was* out there. A primal fear crept up my spine. "Are they watching us now?"

Reagan released my arm to clutch his silver cross, kissing it. Too wary to move forward or retreat, we stood frozen in the silence. Only after the sunlight had completely faded and the chill of night set in did I suggest to Reagan, in a low voice barely above a whisper, that we cautiously make our way back to camp.


"The little shit deserves to die!" Sergeant Darrow bellowed, glaring at Private Rivers who was writhing and screaming on a flat rock. Bud and Fowler strained to hold him still enough for Bud to stitch the deep gashes.

"Keep him down, goddammit!" Bud's hands were slick with blood as he worked the needle through torn flesh. Rivers had erupted into a frenzied panic as soon as he regained consciousness in the woods, and his hysteria hadn't subsided.

By the time Mister Reagan and I returned, Darrow was brandishing his pistol. He wanted blood. He swung the weapon menacingly towards McGinley, who stood her ground, her pistol aimed steadily at him.

"Holster your weapons!" I bellowed.

"That man killed Monte!" Darrow's voice trembled with rage. "By command of the Red Legs, he needs to die!"

"He didn't kill Monte," I countered sharply, gesturing to Mister Reagan to back me up. "Tell him."

Darrow spat on the ground. "The hell you say."

Mister Reagan, pale and shaken, avoided meeting our eyes. His hand clutched his silver cross like a lifeline. His shoulder bled from his gunshot wound, but he did nothing to cover it.

"Tell him, Reagan!" I urged.

"They took him . . . over the ridge," Mister Reagan finally muttered.

"There, you hear that?" I appealed to the group. "Lower your weapons."

But they were deaf to reason. They didn't seem to hear me.

Time slowed. The group went rigid. Darrow and McGinley's pistols remained aimed, their fingers twitching on the triggers, ready to unleash death at the slightest provocation.

Darrow licked his lips. Blinked sweat away from his eyes.

"Fine," he finally grumbled, his voice a low growl. He began to lower his pistol slowly, and McGinley followed suit. He holstered his weapon first.

I saw the sneer before anyone. It was small, almost imperceptible. But a man like Darrow cannot help but be wicked.

As McGinley was holstering her weapon, Darrow seized the moment to draw his pistol again.

There wasn't even time to yell.

I heard the gunshots first.

Only —

They weren't gunshots.

McGinley must have sensed him reaching for his gun. In a swift motion, she reached to her left, her wrist flicking with practiced precision. The crack of her whip rang out, loud as any gunshot. The first lash knocked the gun from Darrow's hand, sending it clattering to the ground. The second lash targeted more personally — snapping viciously between Darrow's legs.

His eyes bulged, wide as saucers, and his mouth formed a perfect, silent 'O'. He doubled over, clutching himself, hopping from foot to foot. The squeal that escaped him was so high-pitched, it would have rivaled the cries of a startled piglet.

"She split meh cock! She split meh cock!" Darrow collapsed, clutching himself as he rolled onto his side. Soon he was whining more than speaking, gibbering nonsense. His goofy tricorn hat fell over his eyes.

Sergeant McGinley, unfazed, calmly coiled her whip and stowed it away. She then confiscated Darrow's pistol, tucking it into her own belt. Casually, she pulled an apple from her pocket, took a bite, and settled herself by the fire. "Yer fine. It's just a hot zinger, is all." She chewed thoughtfully for a moment, then added with a dismissive glance in his direction, "Anyway, I can't snap off a prick you ain't got." She turned her back to him, unconcerned as Darrow was helped to his feet by Mister Reagan, who looped his good arm around him to assist.

As the group's tensions gradually eased, I turned my attention back to Private Rivers. Bud and Fowler had positioned him on his side on the slick rock to better manage his wounds. A large chunk of flesh was missing; the gashes were ragged and brutal. I could tell it was neither the work of a knife nor a gunshot.

Rivers's face was ashen and shiny, his eyes fixed on some distant, unseen point. The morphine had taken hold.

"What happened, Private?" I asked, hoping he could piece together his fragmented memories.

He strained to think. "There was a deer . . . it had its head down . . . I was stalking it . . . Monte interrupted me . . . I was upset. We were arguing . . . I turned away." He swallowed hard and closed his eyes. When he opened them, I saw tears.

Regaining a bit of composure, he continued, his voice growing firmer. "Out of the corner of my eye . . . I saw something . . . it swiped at me . . . collided with him . . . lifted him off the ground."

"What was he wearing? What kind of uniform?"

He shook his head, frustrated. "Didn't have . . . nothing on."

"Tell me something. Anything you can remember."

"It was tall."

"*It?* How tall?"

"Bigger . . . than us. Couple feet taller."

"It lifted him up. Then what?"

"The thing . . ." He searched my eyes. "Carried him away, sir."

"How?"

"It just . . . did."

There was a tense pause. "A panther," I suggested. "You saw a panther." I turned to the others. "I've seen wild cats as big as any man pick up a soldier with their jaws."

"No!"

"How do you know?" I pressed.

"It . . . put Monte . . . over its shoulder. It stood . . . on two legs." His voice was a dry whisper. "Like us."

"It was dark, Private. You were startled by the ambush. The shadows played tricks on you —"

"— but —"

"A bear, then. A grizz standing is more than eight feet. It had him by the arm, in its jaw." I paused. "That's all it was."

Rivers sat up, summoning strength. "No! I'm telling you — it wasn't a man." Then, softer: "And no animal neither."

"Captain." Bud interjected, pointing at Rivers's short, tightly coiled hair. A shock of gray had appeared, starting over his right eye and extending around the side of his head.

Had it been there before? Even earlier that day?

I couldn't be sure.

"What if," Bud suggested quietly, pulling me aside, "he's telling the truth?"

We fell into silence. "It was a wild cat," I said. "An animal. Possibly a soldier, I'll grant you that. But nothing more."

"We can prove it." Fowler said. We turned to him. "Whatever it was, we can see for ourselves."

"How so?"

He was already loading his weapon.

"Everything leaves a track," he said.


Guided by the light of one of the salvaged wagon lanterns, I led Fowler and McGinley up the gentle slope that separated the lake from the forest. We followed a less challenging path this time, but the dense fog that enveloped us thickened the air with unease, limiting our vision to mere feet ahead. Every footfall produced a sense of dread; each penetration deeper into the woods caused my insides to wince, as if I were betraying some better instinct.

Yet, I remembered, you've felt this fear many times going into battle. And you're still alive.

Yes, I was still alive. I knew I was, with every step, every breath, every heartbeat that landed in my throat.

We reached the clearing.

The fog had thinned out by then and lay closer to the ground. I could see the trees around us now. I walked to the spot where we'd glimpsed the spill of Monte's blood. Still there.

Fowler took the lantern and began scanning the ground, but the debris of twigs, pine cones, and leaves obscured any definitive prints. The light drizzle that had started didn't help; it dampened the moss, making our task harder.

"It *was* big," he said, venturing deeper into the dense dogwood as he swept the lantern's light over the ground. I heard the whoosh of a match as McGinley lit up a marijuana cigarette. Her fingers shook, her lips tight and face drawn.

We pushed through to a larger area where we could stand upright. Fowler paused, his back to me, peering into what seemed like an abyss of dense foliage.

"Lieutenant?" I called out, the rain now a steady presence, dripping from his headwrap.

"The private's right," he said. "Monte was carried through here. He was unconscious. Out in a blink."

"Do you see animal tracks?"

"No, sir." He looked away. Seemed like he didn't want to disappoint me. "It wasn't a bear. And no panther either."

"Another soldier, then."

"No."

"Then what?"

With a sweep of his hand, he swept aside a fern, lowering the lantern to illuminate the ground. The soil there was nearly untouched except for one peculiar detail.

I examined the footprint.

If you could call it that.

It had five distinct toe marks, but as I traced the outline, my eyes caught a sixth toe, abnormally long and connected by what seemed to be webbed flesh.

I set my boot next to it. The print was a good three inches longer and half again as wide.

Kneeling for a closer look, I met Fowler's eyes.

Neither of us spoke. Didn't need to.

We both found the talon marks disquieting at best.

"Men who are not men," he said.

# CHAPTER 9

By the following morning the rain had stopped. Morning sun reflected off the shiny grass, edging the lake in sparkling emerald. Critters of the dawn — jackrabbits, songbirds, squirrels — scurried happily from their nests, offering relief from the despondency of the previous night.

As the crew gathered for morning coffee, Darrow emerged from his tent somewhat sheepishly, eyeing his surroundings cautiously as if expecting another whip-crack from McGinley. He seemed to be walking fine; apparently her claim to have merely brushed his manhood was correct.

With everyone assembled, I briefed Darrow and Mister Reagan on our findings from the night before.

"What was it?" Darrow asked. "An injun?" He shot a pointed look at Fowler. "One of your breed?"

"No injun made that footprint," Fowler said.

"'Course they did." Darrow fished a wad of tobacco from inside his cheek and threw it onto the fire's coals, where it sizzled. "They're just wearing boots to frighten us. Seen it myself in Chippewa territory." He nodded with finality. "Men there draped bear skins around 'em, slapped some kinda injun boot on to terrify the whites."

They began to argue. I let it happen; I needed to think by myself for a moment.

I recalled a time during my second stint as a private when our unit, led by the nervous Captain Jenkins, became stranded in a swamp behind enemy lines. With only two days' worth of food, and little game to hunt, the men quickly became unruly and unresponsive. When it became apparent that Captain Jenkins could no longer provide a coherent plan, the unit unraveled quickly.

Something unspoken passed darkly from man to man. A breakdown of command, of authority, and everyone knew it. In dark corners, we began to plot. There was snickering. Mocking laughs. As the captain's nerves deteriorated, so did his authority. Orders went unanswered, posts stood unguarded.

One day, Captain Jenkins went off into the forest to relieve himself, followed discreetly into the woods by three men.

He never returned.

The lesson was this: There is no room in war for a fickle captain. Even my crew could become unruly. As much as I trusted them, they could be persuaded in extremis to abandon ship. One must project confidence.

This memory sharpened my resolve.

"Listen," I said, "the road behind us is gone. Our only path is forward, past the outpost. We're not dealing with ghosts or phantoms but perhaps a few stray Confederates. We've faced worse. We still have our mission, our ammunition, and each other. We're an elite team, prepared for anything."

I ordered the camp to be broken down. We needed to move, to maintain momentum. Doubt, like an unchecked wound, would fester and weaken us all.

But even as I packed, the echoes of last night's discovery lingered, nagging at me. What if this was the wrong move? Where *had* Monte been taken?

And what the hell did Jacob have to do with all this?

# CHAPTER 10

We found the outpost deserted. The gate lay open. Left in haste.

The formidable twenty-foot walls encased a central parade ground where a solitary water well sat, its bucket abandoned in the dirt. Flanking the parade ground were two cabins, with a third facing the entrance directly. Nearby, an outdoor stable, its dry brown hay a phantom of better days, sat beside the left cabin. Shoddily constructed revetments of tree trunks shored up the walls, forming a square perimeter about two hundred feet on each side — a simpler layout than a strategic star shape.

At each corner, platforms surveyed the area. They were connected by elevated walkways that allowed movement above ground around the outpost. On the southwest platform rested a Drummond light, or limelight, used for blinding enemies, with another stationed on the north walkway. Dust-coated Gatling guns stood sentinel on the west walkway and southeast corner, their ammunition wheels fully loaded yet untouched.

We crunched over weeds as we moved forward. Dirt claimed everything. Shovels and pickaxes lay discarded and half-buried. I wondered if the well water was still good or if we'd be burdened with finding refreshment elsewhere.

I signaled McGinley and Fowler to flank me as we approached the rear cabin. I split the rest into two teams: Bud and Private Rivers, and Darrow and Mister Reagan, each tasked with securing the remaining cabins.

The rear cabin interior was so dusty I had to pause a moment and look around, making sure nothing was moving except the particles shimmering in the air. I swept the area from left to right with my rifle. The others followed suit as they entered behind me.

Chairs were kicked over, a bookcase had fallen, a mostly empty table held a few plates and what looked like the remnants of chicken bones. Hard to tell, under those dark layers of writhing maggots.

Then —

*Creeaaaak.*

I motioned with my gun to the others. The noise was coming from upstairs. Cautiously, I approached the staircase, sidestepping a scatter of papers.

*Creeaaaak.*

My gaze darted upward, probing the darkness. Placed one foot timidly on the first step and then —

I ascended.

Reaching the top, I pressed myself against the wall, pivoting my rifle toward the noise.

A figure sat in a wooden chair, back turned to me.

"Turn," I commanded.

Only the back of a head with short hair was visible, dimly lit by a sliver of light from a small open window. The room remained in shadow.

"Turn or be shot," I said louder.

The figure stirred slightly, as if wriggling.

That's when I saw it.

Edging closer, rifle at the ready, I reached out and touched the shoulder. Abruptly, a crow burst forth from the man's face, its beak having been deep in the eye socket, dropping whatever it found there as it squawked and fled through the window. I recoiled, my boot catching on a loose floorboard, sending me to my knees with a shock.

Fowler hooked an arm under mine and pulled me up. He offered a smile, but I could tell it was false.

I nodded — *I'm fine* — then together with McGinley, we turned the chair to face us.

The corpse's eyes were gone, devoured. It seemed the crow had been harvesting what it could from the remains — likely bits of brain. The flesh had decayed to the bone. My gaze fell to the brown jacket with a close-range bullet hole, singed black at the edges.

I pushed the chair back. A pistol rested on the floor. It appeared the man had shot himself in the chest.

Fowler struck a match, casting a small sphere of yellow light.

Surveying the scene, I noted the desk, a couple of dressers, and a bed mildewed and too short for any normal man. The closet held a few uniforms; I brushed my hand across the wool jackets and cotton shirts, feeling the textures.

Nothing unusual, nothing to indicate what might have happened to the outpost.

"How long you reckon since this man met St. Peter?" I asked, gesturing to the deceased.

"The body doesn't stink," Fowler said. "Whatever happened here has long passed."

I jumped as McGinley slammed the dresser door shut. "Goddamn degenerates left nothing for us."

Ignoring her frustration — I had no interest in looting the dead — I opened the small window, poking my head out to call to the others below. They had finished their searches.

"Find anything?"

Bud shook his head. "No, sir."

"Mister Reagan?" I raised my voice as he and Darrow approached from the third cabin. "Anything at all?"

He shook his head slowly, seeming distant.

It was around two in the afternoon, and other than the crow that had picked at the unidentified man in the chair, there was no sign of life.

Gathering everyone in the parade ground, I speculated, "It's possible the men who were supposed to work the mine took off with whatever gold they found. There might've been a skirmish, a battle over it. Some survived, some died. Others fled."

"And the unlucky son of a bitch who shot himself upstairs?" McGinley interjected.

I shrugged. "Maybe there was a dispute, and he figured the rebels would kill him anyway. Chose to go out on his own terms. Against overwhelming odds, can't say I wouldn't do the same."

I unfolded the map, scanning it briefly. "The mine is less than a mile west." Peering up, I gauged the sun's position. "Got plenty of daylight left. What you say we trek over and see what all the fuss is about?"

# CHAPTER 11

A man should always trust his guts.

Intuition, given to us by God or nature, is there for a reason. It might tell you to pursue a woman, avoid an alleyway, make an investment, whatever.

You never quite know if it'll be the right decision. You just act. If it turns out to be wrong, well, you deal with it later.

As we were circling the outpost, ready to head uphill to the mine, every instinct I had shouted at once.

Turn around, they said. Take your men and run. Go down the mountain. Doesn't matter which way. Just go now. With any luck you'll make it to some town on the other side.

I tell you, every bone in my body begged me to do it.

But I was good at ignoring them back then, see? I'd been doing it for eighteen years — so I didn't think much of that inner voice that screamed at me from time to time. I had made it this far, hadn't I?

Why stop then?


We reached the summit and looked out over a colossal pit a few hundred feet across. If you haven't seen a mine before, it's just a giant hole in the earth. This one had tiered ridges that formed paths, useful for moving equipment or navigating the depths without the need to scale the steep sides directly.

Tentatively, we made our way down the carved zig-zag path towards the three tunnel entrances embedded in the far side of the pit, about two-thirds of the way down.

Leading the descent, I noticed the air becoming cooler and damper, the sounds from above growing fainter. Scattered along our path were abandoned tools and brittle sifting troughs, their cracked beds telling of long disuse. Over my shoulder, I caught Darrow discreetly pocketing a hand grenade he'd unearthed, a Ketchum. Possibly a three-pounder, it looked undamaged, the tailpiece not even bent.

Reaching the opposite side, I signaled to Bud, who promptly prepared torches he'd pre-soaked in pitch tar back at the outpost. With torches lit, we entered the nearest tunnel.

About ten feet wide, the tunnel was framed by timber supports, creating an almost cathedral-like structure overhead. The path here was more refined, with metal tracks embedded into the ground. A discarded handcart lay tipped against the wall, its frame tangled in cobwebs.

A colder dampness enveloped us, intensifying the deeper we went. The air tasted faintly of metal, and with each step into the bowels of the earth, I couldn't shake the feeling we were entering some alien throat, soon to be digested by an ungodly creature.

We pressed forward, undeterred.

The metallic rails underfoot eventually ended, giving way to a rough, natural passage that widened into a small chamber. Ahead, two narrower tunnels branched off, their ragged, unbraced walls suggesting they were not carved by human hands but were natural geological formations.

As I paused to consider our path, a faint moan issued from somewhere in the darkness beyond.

"Fuck —"

"Quiet!" I whipped around to hush whoever had spoken.

The flickering torchlight cast uneasy shadows as we listened intently, but the moan did not repeat. Gathering our nerves, we proceeded in single file through the tighter, more oppressive tunnel. Despite the cold, the heat from my torch beaded sweat on my brow.

Several minutes passed before the tunnel opened. We emerged into a large cavern with high ceilings. Someone behind me gagged as I discovered the rancid, putrefactive scent for myself. Horrendous body odor, combined with a rotting, unidentified decay, conspired to nearly send me to the floor. Private Rivers couldn't contain himself, and retched loudly.

We tied handkerchiefs around our noses and mouths to filter the stench, then continued carefully along the cavern wall, the air thick and malodorous.

Our torchlight flickered against the cavern's walls, illuminating ancient drawings. Faded sketches depicted what looked to be men engaged in primitive scenes of conflict and survival against giant wolves and woolly mammoths. A winged creature, unidentifiable and ominous, soared above a battlefield strewn with dead figures lying horizontally.

I squinted at the next series of paintings. Two hunched figures were strangely contorted, one bent over the other, apparently in the midst of a sexual act. The elongated member of the first figure snaked between the legs of the second, ending at the abdomen.

Fowler ran his left hand across the wall. Something caught under his fingertip. Curious, he leaned in, pulling the torch nearer for better illumination, and carefully dug his fingernails under the object lodged in the rock. With a bit of effort, it sprang loose. Holding it close to the light, he examined his discovery.

A mangled bullet.

Suddenly, Bud's urgent voice echoed from deeper within the cavern. "Captain!"

I turned, his torchlight beckoning from afar.

"Look . . ." He pointed to the wall. My hand brushed against it, feeling something amiss. The crumbly dirt flaked away under my touch.

Running my hands over it, I felt the earth give way, uncovering vertical wooden bars hidden behind a thin layer of dirt. It looked like a crude jail cell.

A hideous figure lunged at me from the darkness within.

"Help meeee!" A hand shot out through the bars, grabbed my wrist with unexpected strength, and yanked me violently toward the hole. I screamed, struggling against the man's grasp as he pulled me into the shadows.

As I fought to free myself, the flicker of our torches illuminated his face.

Monte.

Only a day had passed since his disappearance, yet the change was grotesque. Half his scalp had been torn away; a pancake of flesh and hair slapped against his skull. His left eye, punctured, jellied in its socket like a deflated balloon. His nose was missing, revealing a horrific visage as his torn lips fluttered, exposing a few remaining teeth. He babbled endlessly, his one good eye squirming in its socket.

"Back away," I croaked to what was once Monte, finally wrenching my hand free. I nodded sharply to Bud, who readied his axe. "Get him out."

He swung once, twice. The wooden jail bars were heavy and sturdy, and would take some time to breach.

As he banged away, the chopping echoing through the expansive cavern, I felt a sense of panic as I pondered the obvious question:

Who had stuck Monte in this cell?

That ancient, primal instinct surged within me. I felt the sensation of unseen eyes watching.

Was this the fear that had haunted prehistoric men, crouched in their caves, wary of the night's shadows?

The axe continued to fall, and with each beat the unnamed terror drew closer. I felt its steady advance, though I still saw nothing.

I set a hand on Bud's shoulder, signaling him to pause.

The rest of the group, sensing the shift in the air, drew closer together, forming a tight circle.

I waved my flame, casting its light perhaps twenty feet. I bargained with myself. Maybe nothing would enter this protective ring.

I edged forward for a better look. Then a skittering sound echoed through the cavern, claws on stone, something retreating from our encroaching light.

"Father, don't hurt him!" Monte's screams clanged about our ears like church bells portending doom. "He didn't take the money! Bleed me instead! I did it! I took it!"

Sergeant McGinley slammed her fist against the bars. "Shut up!"

In the dimness beyond our light, the sound of scuttling feet continued. Huddling even tighter, our group heeled backward in unison. As we did, the torches created a stronger illumination that extended farther into the cave.

We saw the dozens of faces, eerily smooth, like rocks worn down by centuries of flowing water. Their snouts were long and angular, with jagged teeth protruding aggressively. The eyes, large and oddly set, watched us from different directions.

The creatures stood upright, towering at seven or eight feet tall, their large, distorted bodies ending in what seemed like vaguely human genitalia. My stomach churned as I noticed the viscous, yellow-green pus dripping from them, the sight exacerbating the already foul smell filling the air.

I stretched a hand behind me, signaling the crew to fall back.

*Steady. Steady now.*

We clustered together, our weapons and torches at the ready as we retreated. I stutter-stepped backward, my shaky legs somehow propping me up, as the beings shielded their faces from our torches. Hundreds, perhaps thousands, of years of darkness, of living underground, had left them vulnerable to our brand of brightness.

Now, beyond the hiss of the flame, I heard the wheezing of the humanoids. Their snouts, long and nasty, were producing large swaths of mucus, distorting their breathing. Amid my fear, I sensed some kind of illness within them. They followed us but, strangely, showed no sign of attacking.

*Step. Pause. Step. Pause.*

I glanced behind us. We would soon reach the tunnels. I had no plan for what we'd do then.

As I looked back at the humanoid crowd, something on the edge of my vision caught my attention.

The face flickered in and out of view. I squinted. Unlike the other figures, this one had no snout. Its eyes and mouth were misaligned, creating a disturbing visage.

A flicker of recognition stirred within me.

Could it be . . .?

I ceased to breathe.

*No.*

It couldn't be.

The dancing flames shifted the light.

I blinked, and the face was gone in the darkness.

"Captain?" Lieutenant Fowler called. He was watching Sergeant Darrow, who had caught the attention of one particular humanoid. I saw the fear in his eyes and heard it in the whimper that escaped him.

This humanoid was taller than the others, with a snout scarred as if by a giant porcupine. Its face looked weathered and beaten. Its nails clicked on the ground, increasing in speed as its breathing quickened. It was clearly growing excited. It smiled.

And I smelled the unholy motive in the odor the thing emitted; it was foul and stank of old urine, but I knew in my bones what it was.

This was a scent of seduction in their world.

The beast had chosen him.

Darrow watched in galloping terror, covering his crotch, which seemed to excite the beast more. It grinned, revealing green teeth and a thick, shiny, spore-laden tongue inside a blackened mouth.

The tongue waggled with delight.

The creature's eyes narrowed as it shifted, grotesquely flaunting its sex. Ooze dripped from the pubic area, and the distended outer lips throbbed. The air thickened with a heavy, unspoken tension.

In that moment, Sergeant Darrow's instinct kicked in. Before I could intervene, he had pulled the grenade from his pocket.

I reached out, shouting for him to stop.

But it was too late.

With a deft flick of his wrist, Darrow hurled the grenade over the heads of the humanoids.

I had just enough time to cup my ears and fall to the ground before the plunger of the grenade hit the rock and everything exploded into yellow and white.

I had survived many explosions, but none as disorienting as this, and in such an enclosed space. The detonation sent shockwaves through my skull, my vision blurred, and a grotesque mist of blood and gore spattered across me like a gruesome sneeze. A crushing pressure exploded in my ears, plunging me into a hollow silence. I sensed a warm, sticky trickle — blood — seeping from my ears.

I shouldered my rifle and grabbed the nearest soldier by the uniform. Gradually, my troops began to raise their heads, alarmed by my screams and frantic gestures, urging them to move.

Time to go.

As slow as we might have been to recover, the humanoids were slower. The blast had thrown them into both stupor and panic. Chaos reigned. In their world of shadows, the sudden, fierce light of the explosion was like an assault by some furious deity.

We scrambled into the tunnel system. In that moment, we were no longer soldiers with ranks or histories. There were no commands to follow, no masters to serve. It was about survival — nothing more. Society, wealth, family — all were meaningless. In our horror, we regressed back down the evolutionary ladder, to a primordial time, when violence made a jest of brotherhood; when humans were not human, when we languished in the ooze of the swamp. When out of sheer will to survive, we leapt onto land and climbed up our first tree to escape the long-fanged, drooling creatures who hunted on crumbling ledges over bottomless pits. To a time when dawn was a distant dream, when mothers devoured their young, when magic ruled the world.

I came out of my vision and almost shrieked with joy. The tunnel ahead was growing lighter. I saw a hint of daylight and accelerated towards it. Just before reaching the tunnel's end, my foot caught on a half-buried canister of kerosene. Stumbling but catching myself, I let the others rush ahead as I seized the torch from Private Rivers's grasp.

I darted back to retrieve the kerosene, shaking it. Mostly full. Unscrewing the cap, I tipped it over, letting the flammable liquid spill across the tunnel floor.

A distant roar snapped my focus back to the shadows advancing in the tunnel. As they drew closer, their forms barely visible in the dim light, I backed away, waiting for the perfect moment.

With a flick of my wrist, I hurled the torch into the spilled kerosene and bolted into the light.

*WHOOSH!*

The screams that followed were unlike any horror conceived by nature or nightmare. Flaming figures slipped and fell, tumbling out of the tunnel and into the pit. I was already sprinting along the pit's edge, shouting triumphantly as my pursuers writhed in agony.

Daylight, though, was fading fast. The sky reddened and night descended with each lunge closer to the outpost as I made my way back into the forest.

I ran close to the ground, driven by a wild fear, as my toe caught on a rock. Arms flailing, I barely kept my balance. A sharp pain shot through my foot; I'd broken a toe, which slowed me for a moment. It was then, amidst the quieting chaos, that I heard a distant voice calling my name from back towards the mine.

"Nathaniel!"

I whipped around, my heart pounding, trying to pinpoint the source of the scream. To my astonishment, the path behind me was empty — no sign of the beasts I was certain were on my heels.

Ahead, my troops were sprinting toward the fort, figures blurring in the distance. Gasping for breath, I bent over, hands on my knees, as sweat streamed down my face. My clothes clung to my body, soaked through.

"Captain!" The call came again, this time unmistakably from the direction of the outpost. It was Bud. He must have thought I was lost, or worse, captured. If I didn't show myself soon, he'd risk coming back for me, a risk I couldn't let him take.

I strained my ears, waiting for another call from the unknown voice, as I faced westward. The path I'd crested over uphill fell off seemingly into nothing. The sun was now just a memory below the horizon, casting a hostile red-orange glow across everything.

Silence.

I hobbled on, limping. I reached the outpost. As Bud greeted me at the gate, we quickly slammed and secured it behind us. And there, carried faintly on the wind as the gate clanged shut, was the voice again. It sounded as if it were struggling through a disfigured, crooked throat, calling out to me.

I suspected who it was.

I reckoned what he wanted.

My brother.

Revenge.

# CHAPTER 12

The outpost came under attack within minutes of my arrival.

I stepped inside as Bud slid two heavy wooden beams across the slats, securing the door from within. The rest of the team was already in motion, setting up our defenses. Mister Reagan and Sergeant Darrow hustled the first Gatling gun up the ramp to cover the western approach, while in their wake Fowler and Private Rivers lugged a crate of shells.

Bud and McGinley positioned the second gun on the southwest platform. While a frontal assault from the west seemed most likely, we couldn't risk leaving any side of the fort unprotected. Besides, the mobility of the Gatling guns allowed for quick repositioning as needed.

*What would we need next?*

The Drummonds.

Limping, each step sending shock waves through my right leg, I gritted my teeth and lunged forward, yelling for Bud to help me on the next platform to set up the lights.

"Here they come!" Lieutenant Fowler's voice boomed across the outpost.

On his platform, Darrow stumbled, steadying himself against the Gatling gun. Mister Reagan stood with dual pistols aimed, ready to fire. Fowler and Rivers, unfamiliar with how to light the Drummonds, resorted to their rifles for the time being. McGinley had just finished loading the second Gatling gun.

I cupped my hands around my mouth and bellowed, "Fire at will!"

350 rounds per minute shredded the forest.

I let my crew work while I hustled up the platform for the first Drummond. The pale moonlight and the yellow blaze from the Gatling guns cast an eerie glow, creating surreal silhouettes of Darrow and Reagan against the canopy overhead.

Reaching the platform's top, I looked over the wall — and gasped.

"God almighty."

Dozens of humanoids were darting between the trees, quickly encircling us. My men fired wildly. I clamped a hand on Private Rivers's shoulder, urging him to conserve ammo where he could. His glazed eyes, wide and unseeing, chilled me. Fowler was more disciplined, firing only at clear targets.

Our shrieking bullets tore apart the humanoids' smooth flesh. One took a hit straight through its snout as it faced Bud. Its head jerked back as its skull shattered on impact, brains splattering across the feet of its companions.

Kneeling, I flipped open the hatch of the Drummond light and sighed in relief to see the calcium oxide ball already loaded. Then I descended the steps, grabbed the last burning torch — fortunately left upright in the soil — and staggered back up.

Just as the humanoids burst from behind the trees like jesters in a carnival parade, I ignited the calcium oxide. The Drummond light blazed to life, casting a fierce, blinding light across the forest. Night turned to day.

Their screeches competed with the cacophony of the gunfire; the intense light seared their atrophied senses, halting them midsprint as though they'd hit an invisible wall. Amid the chaos, Fowler accidentally turned and caught the light. Shrieking, he collapsed and covered his eyes, his rifle clattering to the deck.

Pulling Rivers close, I directed him to take over the Drummond light, which he did smoothly, dropping his rifle. Meanwhile, Darrow and Reagan relentlessly pummeled the forest, unleashing a storm of bullets. I glanced to my left, checking on Bud and McGinley, who were also decimating any movement they could.

I wanted to help Fowler, but I needed to act. I saw that the creatures were beginning a calculated shift to the sides of the outpost that we hadn't fortified. I limped across the parade ground, ascended the north-facing platform, and activated the other Drummond light, just as the bastards launched their renewed assault.

One beast leapt toward the wall, trying to scale it. I angled the light downwards. The blast of molten yellow-white hit it straight on; I could almost see its scorched retinas begin to smoke under the glare. The eyes bugged out, a look of disbelief washed across its face, and it plummeted to the ground where it bawled and crawled away blindly in despair.

Glancing east, I saw McGinley spin her gun and shred four of the beasts to tatters — limbs flailing, torsos wrecked. To the west, Darrow and Reagan quickly switched to a fresh ammo wheel.

Between the two lights and guns, we somehow held the fort. One after another, the humanoids retreated back into the forest.

This was it. We were going to win.

But just when victory seemed within reach, chaos erupted again.

Rivers, temporarily abandoning the light, rushed to aid Fowler, who, blinded and disoriented, had backed against the wall. Rivers drew his pistol just as a creature, having evaded our lights and gunfire and scaled the twenty-foot wall, reached over and seized Fowler by the head. He fired, hitting the beast, but by then it was too late.

The claws dug into Fowler's forehead and tore the scalp away from front to back. My lieutenant went over the parapet's edge like a child's stick toy, lifeless before he hit the dirt.

Rivers roared. As did I. And Bud, and McGinley.

We who have been in war and fought together know that in the heat of battle, there is no sadness and no victory, no joy and no defeat. There is only rage and terror, often intertwined.

We redoubled our efforts. A new fury overtook me. It was no longer enough to blind these creatures; I wanted to taste their suffering. I needed not only to survive, but to see them exterminated, wiped from this earth. Whatever they were — human or otherwise — they did not deserve to breathe.

The ground before us was littered with fallen bodies as the horde dwindled. The Gatling guns, now stuttering, fired in controlled bursts, nearly spent of their ammunition.

"Look! Look at 'em go!" Darrow stamped on the platform.

Yes. There was no way to tell how many were left, but they retreated into the woods by twos and threes, shielding their faces and stumbling back into the shadows from which they had emerged.

Then —

Something else caught my eye.

A figure stood some fifty yards away, stoically observing from behind an oak tree. While the humanoids dashed past in their retreat, this figure remained motionless. I squinted, subtly adjusting the Drummond light to better discern its features.

It had no snout; that much was clear.

It wasn't a humanoid.

No.

This figure was human.

Moments stretched as I watched, nearly hypnotized, until the figure's outline blurred and merged with the trees, and I could no longer separate my vision from my mind's eye.

A cheer erupted from Bud. Then McGinley. Rivers.

I blinked, came out of my trance. The Gatling guns fell silent. I watched as the last of the beasts withdrew. Whether this was a genuine defeat or a ploy to lower our defenses, I couldn't say. At that moment, I hardly cared.

I searched again for the figure among the trees, but, false vision or not, it had disappeared. All that remained on our little battlefield were the mangled bodies of torn half-men, men who were not men, the dregs of the tunnels.

We had fought them, and for a brief moment, victory was ours. But I knew it would be a fleeting triumph. At best, we had stayed them for the night and the following day.

At worst, they would regroup and return with a more cunning and devilish plan.

But they wouldn't attack again that night.

We all whooped and hollered for our success.

As the night deepened and the joy waned, my thoughts returned to the figure in the trees. The voice calling for me hadn't been a figment of my imagination. I knew who it was.

Jacob was alive. And he knew I had come for him.

I thought of telling the others. About Jacob, and who he was to me. What I had tried to do to him in his crib.

Of course, I did. But what good would it do? Revealing our relationship would only complicate the mission and possibly undermine my command, risking the trust of my troops. So, I talked myself out of it.

Yet, deep down, I knew the real reason for my silence was something else entirely.

The unspeakable thing.

I couldn't face it.

# CHAPTER 13

Dawn came.

We huddled around the blazing fire in the parade ground, secure that the somewhat sunny morning afforded enough protection for us to come down off our platforms and take stock of how much supplies and ammunition we had left.

Fowler's death weighed heavily upon us. We recovered his body near the outer wall. For what it was worth, what remained of his face held some measure of peace. I prayed the half-breed had transitioned smoothly to the other side.

"We have our pistols, with plenty of rounds," I said. "A rifle for each of us, three hand grenades, and we still have lime for the Drummond lights. But we're nearly out of shells for the Gatling guns." I turned to Mister Reagan. "What's left of our food?"

He fingered the cross around his neck, his gaze lost in the fire. "Days, few days, two days, fuckin' cares . . .."

I had thought giving him a job might bring back his mind. Apparently, it had not.

Private Rivers changed direction. "How long until we can expect Price to send another crew?"

"A rescue mission, you mean?" I said. "We *are* the rescue mission. We can't assume anyone's coming for us." I laid the map out on the ground. "West is the only way off this mountain. Fowler had said it's slow going, might take eight or nine days. But —"

"Nine fuckin' days!" Darrow interrupted, leaping to his feet. He gesticulated toward the two horses we had left — the only ones lucky enough to have been secured in the fort during the attack. "Two of us can go! Take the animals and blaze out of here, put miles between us and them by nighttime. Get help and bring 'em back. That's my vote."

"And I suppose you'd be the one blessed enough to go, eh?" McGinley was winding her whip around her hand, hat cocked to one side.

"Why not me? All you's done since we set off on this goddamned fuckfest is get us killed!"

"It would take too long," I said. "Nine days to get off the mountain, find Price, gather another willing crew, and return. We're talking about weeks, a month, maybe longer. In the meantime, those staying would have no horses, nothing to . . . eat if things get dire. No, we stay together, leave together."

"We're not gonna get anywhere on foot!" Darrow spat.

"Hunt us down like dogs by next dawn," Mister Reagan blurted out, his tricorn hat askew.

I turned to Bud. "Penny for your thoughts?"

He wiped the sweat from his forehead. The tremors were back. He shook his head. *I don't know.*

"McGinley?" I prompted.

She drew a breath, took her time to buckle her whip to her belt, and peered out from under the brim of her hat. I saw fire there. "Way I see it, there's little chance of any of us walking outta here for long. Don't matter if we have horses or not. Don't matter when we leave, or what we leave with. Those things own this place and everything around it. While we're discussing our exit, one of their crew is with them right now." Her eyes flicked toward the cave, clearly thinking of Monte.

Were these the choices the first group had had to make? Was this how the inevitable decline had begun for them? Deciding whether to run or stay?

Death by combat or attrition?

Which was worse?

Sooner or later, I knew our hand would be forced. The siege would tighten; driven by fear and hunger, we'd run. Weakened, we wouldn't last long.

Then, the idea came. The dreadful idea. The very thought of it nearly broke me. As I faced my troops, acceptance settled in heavily.

But, I realized, there was no way around it.

I sighed, removed my hat, and sat down by the fire.

"It's time I was honest with you all," I began, and laid everything bare: the attempted murder eighteen years ago, my flight from Ironwood, the connections drawn from MacReady's supposed delusions to the reality that the man leading these savages was my brother, Jacob Carter. I admitted to hearing his voice on the wind, to seeing him among the trees the night before.

He was alive, and he might be our only hope for survival.

"Maybe, if I can talk to him, I can negotiate for us," I proposed. "They've accepted him as one of their own; perhaps they'll let us go, too."

Darrow's mouth was catching flies in disbelief. McGinley shifted uncomfortably. Bud and Private Rivers, too, inspected me from the corners of their eyes.

Then, Mister Reagan erupted with a sudden, uproarious laugh that startled us all. His tricorn hat shifted comically as he rocked with uncontrollable laughter, wobbling on his tree-stump seat. Tears streamed down his face, and then, abruptly, he toppled backward, flattening his hat in the dirt. His laughter turned to spasms. A wet stain darkened his trousers, spreading rapidly until it soaked through to his boots. A wet fart then issued from him. Judging by the smell, I suspected something else had, too.

"Anyone else share Mister Reagan's sentiment?" I asked, raising an eyebrow.

There was a long silence.

McGinley shifted uncomfortably, then cleared her throat. "You never saw him before? Jacob, I mean, all grown up?"

"That's right."

"And he was in the shadows?"

"Yes."

"So how do you know it's really him?"

I hesitated. I tried but couldn't put better words to it. "I just know."

"Sir?" Private Rivers interjected. "I have something to contribute."

"By all means."

"I think we're overlooking something."

"What's that?"

"Well, we can all see that Price blasted away half a mountain. Looking for the gold, right . . .? But where is the gold?"

This gave me pause.

He continued. "At first, I thought some of the first group might have taken it. But no one could have carried all that gold far."

"What are you saying, Private?"

"If the gold is still here, it's obviously somewhere we haven't looked. It could be hidden with weapons, food, supplies. We might be able to hold out in this siege long enough to exterminate these beasts. I'm speaking only for myself, sir, but I don't think we should chance you negotiating with them. I say we fight."

"Where d'ya suppose the gold is? We searched the goddamned houses already," Darrow growled. "Nuffin' in 'em!"

"There's something else." Now Bud found his voice, pushing his glasses up with a shaky hand. "They're taking troops. Kidnapping them as much as killing them. You saw what they did to Monte. They beat him up good, then stripped him down, stuck him in that hole. Why would they do that?" As he spoke, he grew steadier. "We need to know what they're *really* doing. He cleared his throat. "With your permission, sir, I'd like to perform an autopsy."

"You wanna carve one of 'em bastards open?" Darrow said.

"That's right."

"Why?" I asked.

"Anything that can help us understand what we're dealing with should be useful, sir."

Bright morning light filtered through the trees. The birds were loud, and a shiny dew coated every green thing. The day had begun. Maybe things weren't as hopeless as they felt. We didn't have to run. Not yet, anyway. We still had munitions to last us through another night, maybe two. We could sleep in the day, in shifts.

"All right." I gestured to Rivers. "Let's see if there's anything to your gold idea. As for you —" I turned to Bud. "Let's go cut one of these bastards up."

When Bud was thirteen, he'd developed a growing suspicion about his father's nightly activities. He told me how, lying in his bed, he'd hear the soft creak of the stairs and the faint squeak of the front door opening. The kind of noise made by someone trying to be discreet. Curious, he'd sneak to the living room, peek through a crack in the door, and watch his father cross the road and vanish into the tall grass.

So, one night, Bud decided to uncover the secret for himself.

He waited until his father was well into the grass before following. He was careful to avoid the noisy spots on the porch.

The grass gave way to a footpath through the trees, heading north. He was nearing the Healdsburg farm. From behind a maple tree, he watched his father enter a barn with Mister Healdsburg and two other men.

Creeping to the window, he peered inside. Healdsburg was pouring liquid from a large vat into cups, distributing them among the men. Bud's dad took a sip. His tense shoulders dropped, a haze came over his eyes, and it was then that Bud knew — even before tasting it for himself — that alcohol was for him.

Before long, he found his chance. His father, having brought a jug home, tried to hide it on account of their being Baptist and all. It didn't take Bud long to discover where it was kept.

From that moment on, Bud hardly drew a sober breath. What started as a foray into manhood became something else. Something darker. Needier. Many nights in his late teenage years he would simply collapse in the barn; he'd awaken to his father berating him, dismayed and confused at how his son was getting liquor.

And yet, for a while, Bud maintained his status as a high achiever. A gifted man in the sciences, he studied anatomy and became a doctor at twenty-two. For several years he maintained his own practice in a small cottage at the edge of town. At twenty-five he married a fetching woman named Mary Lynch, who tried in vain to persuade him to stop imbibing so much.

In the end, he drank his life into the ground.

Knowing full well he couldn't maintain, and disgusted with himself, he left his marriage and set out on the road to give his life some shape.

I met him in Henrico County, Virginia, during the early days of the war. Our battalion had lost over fifteen hundred men as we were pursued by General John Magruder at Savage's Station. Afterward, he sat next to me on an exploded tree stump, wearing a pilgrim's hat and carrying a haunted look in his eyes.

We became fast friends.

Now, as he stood over the body of the dead humanoid — which had been laid on its back over a table — and slipped on an apron like a doctor's garb, he had a similar look. The tightly drawn mouth. The clenching of the jaw. I wondered if a drink wouldn't do him some good.

He took a deep breath and placed the scalpel on the towel draped over a knee-high wooden bookshelf, then carefully removed the white sheet from the upper half of the humanoid.

It was a loathsome thing, easily seven feet tall. The head, from the back of the skull to the tip of its nose, measured as long as my forearm. Its mouth, filled with green-tinged, pointy teeth, formed a nightmarish grin. The skin was leathery, tightly stretched, with thick veins tracing bizarre patterns down its arms. Even in death, its eyes — open, large, black orbs — brooded with malevolence.

"What do you make of it?" I asked.

He scrutinized the upper half, noting its dense torso. "Looks healthy," Bud remarked. "Doesn't need sunlight like we do, I guess." He continued his inspection, pausing as his hands approached the creature's lower half, covered by a sheet.

He unveiled the lower half of the body.

I felt myself begin to retch.

"God almighty." The words caught in my throat. "What happened to its sex? Is it disfigured?"

Bud winced. Even he, a doctor, couldn't stand the sight of it. "No. See, it has no scars. It was born this way."

"You mean . . ."

"Genetic deficiency, perhaps. Came out malformed." He covered the body. Uncomfortable, disgusted: these were not words bold enough to describe our reactions to the creature's twisted genitalia . . . the shrunken testicles alongside the twisted vulva, and the green excretions slicking the area, just like the ones in the cave.

What did it mean? What could be told about a race of creatures from their discharge?

Bud began his incision meticulously, from the neck down the sternum to the pubis, peeling back the skin to reveal the underlying chest. He paused, picking up a sharpened iron stake found earlier in the courtyard, hesitating as he placed its point against the creature's breastbone.

I handed Bud the hammer. He steadied his grip, striking the stake. The first hit barely made a dent, causing him to adjust. After two more forceful hits, the sternum split open. He set the hammer aside and, grasping the fractured breastbone, pulled apart the ribs with a grunt, revealing the organs inside with a series of sickening cracks.

He examined the lungs, liver, and heart. Seemed to find nothing amiss. That is, until he cut away some piece and held it up.

"What is that?" I asked.

"An organ . . . I think."

"You *think*?"

"I've never seen it before."

"Appendix?" I ventured.

He shook his head and set the organ down. Then, he extracted a long, slippery object that resembled a stomach. It was deep red and mushy, almost disintegrating between his fingers. "Connected to the liver . . ." he mused, slicing into it. Immediately, brown pus oozed from the cut, releasing a foul, stomach-churning stench. Bud recoiled, turned, and vomited, his body convulsing

Lunging for the door, he slipped in his own mess, leaving a gruesome trail across the floor. He managed to hurl the remains of the mysterious organ into the yard before gasping like a drowning man seeking air.

Eventually, he steadied himself, wiped his hands on his apron, and attempted to regain his composure by cleaning his glasses with an air of detachment.

Then he did something that made my heart fall.

Sidestepping the vomit that had pooled beneath us, he trundled on jittery legs to the bookshelf holding a couple dozen molding tomes. He reached behind the books. I heard a clank of glass against wood and then saw the bottle of whiskey as the light glinted off it, the one from our encounter with Creed Sides, the one he'd found in the gangster's saddle bag. He'd been saving it. I imagined he slept better knowing it was in his possession, only an arm's length away at all times.

I hadn't thought he would succumb again. He'd been going so strong.

He puttered back to the table with a sheepish look. Didn't look me in the eye. Unscrewing the cap, he peered deeply into the amber liquid. He stared for a long time, studying it intently before bringing the bottle to his nose and taking a deep whiff.

"Bud."

He shook his head in response. The message was clear: *Do not bother me.* This was between him and whatever was in that bottle. Some secret was held there.

Exhaling, he replaced the cap, screwed it on tight, and set the bottle on the table. He hadn't drunk.

After a great silence, he spoke. His tone was different now, steadier. More confident. Something he'd lost and then regained, perhaps.

"I don't know what they are," he said, his brow furrowed. "They share some characteristics with humans — certain organs, for example, or bipedalism. I would like to explore their brains, though I must admit, I don't have the stomach for it at the moment. But clearly, they're not altogether human. I've never seen or heard of any species like them before."

"Some kind of evolution?" I suggested tentatively.

"You mean Darwin's theory?" he asked, pausing. I nodded, having only a passing familiarity with the concept — that some animals evolved from simpler forms into more complex ones.

"I've kept up with the debates," he continued. "Whether man may have descended from apes or even another creature. While the theory makes sense for animals, I find it more challenging when it comes to humans."

"Why's that?"

He sat in his chair, choosing his words carefully. "Evolution might explain how animals adapt physically. But humans create art, write poetry, solve complex mathematical problems. These things go beyond basic survival needs. Where did these needs come from?"

He paused, pondering. "And there are significant gaps in the fossil record, particularly between apes and humans. It's hard to pinpoint a direct ancestor.

"Then again, we may have been thinking about it wrong. What if evolution isn't always slow and gradual? What if it sometimes leaps forward? Perhaps species can evolve quickly, skipping an intermediary step or two. Like a fish that suddenly starts walking on land because it has to survive outside water."

He gestured to the creature on the table. "Like them. If they're neither fully ape nor human, they might represent a rapid evolutionary burst. Perhaps we even share a common ancestor but our lines diverged at some point."

"You think we might be related?"

"On the evolutionary tree, all life is interconnected," he mused. "But yes, it's possible we were closer once. Imagine, just one step back on that tree, there was a fork in the road — one path led to us and civilization, the other to them and . . . the dark."

His words hung heavy in the blood-stained room. His theory left a knot in my stomach. It was a disturbing suggestion, that amidst all the chaos, there was something larger at work here.

*Men who are not men.*

The words rattled in my brain.

Bud's voice pulled me back from my reverie. "You were right," he said, looking directly at me with a newfound determination. "We need to find Jacob. Whatever these creatures are, we need to understand what they're doing with our men. It might be the only way to negotiate with them."

"You don't suspect cannibalism?"

"I wouldn't call it cannibalism. Not if we're different species. And no, I don't think they're using people for food. They're letting Jacob live, aren't they? They locked up Monte up instead of killing him. And they left Fowler's body on the ground, instead of dragging it away."

"But why?" I asked. "What else would they be using people for?"

Bud seemed suddenly drained, the output of thought sapping his strength as he stared at the covered body before us. "That's what I want to find out. Obviously, Jacob is fulfilling some role in their world. The others, too. I want to know what that is."

As I rubbed my temples, trying to process all this, the outside world abruptly intruded.

Excited shouting erupted from the parade ground. I moved towards the window, my heart speeding as I spotted Private Rivers. He was waving his arms dramatically, his voice carrying through the thin glass as he shouted at us. Beside him, McGinley was practically jumping from the ground, her hand clamped down on her hat.

"The gold! We've found the gold!"

# CHAPTER 14

I peered into the hole in the ground.

Hidden by a hulking plank of wood covered with dirt, it had not been immediately visible on the far side of the parade ground. Private Rivers's instincts had been spot on.

Sunlight unfurled down the earthen ramp. The hole, roughly square, was about ten feet in diameter. Its inner sides were reinforced with planks, forming a sort of crude lining that descended into darkness. The construction looked ancient, the wood aged and damp. A faint, musty smell wafted up. Rusty mining equipment lined the walls.

I ventured in behind Private Rivers. Turning a corner, we came upon a series of rooms with unfinished door frames to our right and left. There were four on either side. Rivers entered the last room on the right, and whisked away a large sheet.

In the light of my wavering torch, I saw a dozen buckets and two large, makeshift wooden trays of gold pebbles and flakes of varying sizes. This must be where they stashed the stuff after washing it, I thought; later, they would reconstitute it into bars or jewelry or perhaps coins for Price's private mint. Who knows what the man could do with such an arsenal. He could buy the government with all that.

Private Rivers leaked a grin.

*The gold remained.*

My mind swam at the amount of wealth. The pile seemed almost otherworldly — a king's ransom just lying there, untouched, waiting. For a fleeting moment, I entertained the thought of betraying Price and dividing the treasure among us. But as my eyes measured the vastness of the heap, reality sank in.

First, there was the logistical nightmare of transporting it all. Our two horses, sturdy as they were, couldn't carry our gear, the gold, and all of us. The sheer weight and bulk of the yellow metal made it impossible for our small crew to manage on our own. And even if we could somehow load the horses to their maximum capacity without breaking them, it would barely make a dent in the yellow stacks we'd found. And then there was the journey back — navigating treacherous terrain with overloaded, unhappy animals was inviting disaster.

No, the gold would remain here, at least until Price could organize a proper expedition. He would need wagons, more men, armed guards to secure and transport the treasure to a place where it could be safely smelted and sold. The dream of instant riches dissolved as quickly as it had appeared, leaving the bitter taste of reality.

I backed out of the room and turned right, walking deeper into the tunnel, but stopped short as I found the path obstructed.

The equipment piled haphazardly in front of the makeshift barrier suggested a hurried attempt at a blockade. I examined it closely. Equipment of all kinds had been stacked on top of each other. The angry tangle of metal looked like a boilermaker's worst nightmare. I shined my torchlight into it. Behind the few feet of crap was a wall. But not made of rock.

I squinted. Cinder blocks and mortar. And lots of it.

"This tunnel *should* lead out to the mine, sir." Private Rivers dusted off his hands and joined me. "It's the easy way of bringing the gold out, rather than over the hill outside."

"So they put this up to keep the beasts from coming back through the tunnels," I concluded.

"Sir."

I craned my neck. McGinley was farther back, near the entrance to the tunnel. Rivers and I joined her in a side room.

She gestured to the floor. Empty cans, trash, dry-as-bones water jugs, and a makeshift bed of rags with about half a dozen pillows were strewn around. "MacReady's work, ya think? This where he holed up until he left?"

"Looks that way," I said. "Probably hid down here, waited till he ran out of food, then took his chances in the forest. It's remarkable he survived as long as he did."

Something bothered me about it, but I couldn't say what exactly.

We went back up top. It was afternoon already, and the warm and wonderful morning's bright blue had faded over with endless clouds. A sharp breeze blew. My good mood withered. Soon we'd have to prepare for the nighttime, for the assault that was sure to come.

The others felt the shift, too. Once the excitement of finding the gold died, attention turned to the menial chores that so quickly become boring in wartime. Shoveling pits for relieving ourselves. Chopping and stacking firewood. Bringing up fresh well water. Cleaning weapons.

Chores help to calm the mind and divert energy that would otherwise be wasted. Sometimes the grind of lowly tasks is all that keeps a man going; it offers the promise of usefulness. Once that goes — usefulness, I mean — I'm convinced everything goes. Health, wealth, mental agility. Everything.

I needed rest. But trying now would be futile. Anyway, I'd once stayed awake for eight days during a series of skirmishes outside Alexandria; between each fight I would command furtive missions to disrupt the enemy's supply lines and divert their goods to our pockets. I could hack it.

But there was something about MacReady's escape that I couldn't shake. I had questions. How had he outrun the beasts down the mountain? Did he have a plan? Was it pure luck?

Perhaps I'd missed something, some key piece of information.

Mister Reagan was pissing against the side of the fort, muttering to himself, as Sergeant McGinley passed behind him carrying an armful of firewood. Darrow was perched on the platform above, staring at her like a cat preparing to pounce. McGinley could handle herself, but there was no need to stoke any unwanted fires. I gave her a new chore that would take her across the compound and away from Darrow.

Bud, meanwhile, was dissecting a new corpse in the cabin. Without the proper tools, he couldn't make much use of the brain, so he'd left the head intact. Presently he was focusing on the groin of this one, and was deep into his dissection of the sex when I entered.

"There *is* something wrong with them," he confirmed, head nearly buried in the body.

"Besides the obvious?"

"Yes. To put it bluntly, their pipes don't work. They're crossed up. They seem to lead nowhere at all, or" — he sliced out a thin piece that resembled a long worm and was about as wide, and held it up — "they're so blocked up with clots as to be useless." He tossed the clot on the table and sat back in the chair. He looked utterly exhausted, but I could tell the work had given him a sense of purpose. His color was better, and he was less shaky.

"They can't procreate, you mean?"

"I'd say not." He wiped his fingers on the sheet over the body, smearing viscera. His hands were nearly dyed red; I doubted any amount of cleaning could restore their natural color. "I checked that one, too," he added, pointing to a second body that had been brought in; it now lay in the corner, covered by a white sheet.

"If they can't procreate," I asked, "wouldn't they die off?"

He shrugged. "Who says they aren't? This might be a complication in their evolution. Birth defects due to generation after generation of inbreeding. At some point, it would catch up to them, biologically."

Yes. I supposed it would.

"I've been thinking," I said, then told him about my confusion about MacReady's escape.

"I was thinking about that, too," he said. "There's something we haven't considered."

"What's that?"

"That he didn't escape. He was allowed to leave."

This gave me pause. It was a simple explanation, and made sense — within reason.

But why, when all the others had been taken alive and kept in the mine, had he been given license to go?

"Because they didn't need him anymore," he said. "He'd fulfilled his purpose. Whatever it was."

Suddenly he sat up like something had bitten him. His eyes were wild and crazy, and a crooked smile spread across his face. "His wounds." The words came out like an epiphany. "MacReady's wounds."

"The claw marks on his side?"

"No!" He shook his head. "I gave him a more thorough examination later, after we placed him in the wagon. I wanted to make sure we hadn't missed anything. His legs were black and blue, and I noticed that his bruises worsened farther up his thighs. It looked as if his adductors had been beaten to a pulp. After the morphine knocked him out completely, I pulled down his pants for a better view.

"He still had his member and testes, though there were several cuts along his penis and around the gracilis muscles. The cuts looked intentional, not like he'd been running through the forest and been tripped up on some brambles or bushes. No, these were done *on purpose.*

"It could hold a clue, couldn't it?"

It could. But every clue seemed to produce more questions.

I felt as though there was a solution on the tip of my tongue.

"Good work," I told him, "let's keep it going." I walked out, moseying outside, my thoughts still on the subject at hand. Without realizing it, I had looped the parade ground several times, when —

"Sir! Someone approaches!" Private Rivers was at the lookout tower, whistling to get my attention.

I didn't know it then, but a chain of events was about to occur that would answer all of my questions.

In the worst way.

CHAPTER 15

As the sun dipped toward the horizon, I shielded my eyes to better see the figure shambling towards us from the direction of the mine. The silhouette was gangly, skeletal.

We were stationed defensively on our platforms and walkways. I called Bud out to help man the weapons; he, McGinley, and I faced west, while Darrow, Private Rivers, and Mister Reagan covered the south and northwest. The front gate was securely closed and barred; in my quick assessment I could see no other countermeasures to take.

The silhouetted man — for I could plainly see it was no woman — was stumbling forward as if driven by thirst through a desert. His legs continued to move in an automatic fashion; some wind-up doll continuing his programming. His head bowed toward the dirt; he wasn't looking where he was going.

As the sun's glare lessened behind the trees, though, I could see him more clearly.

He was stark naked, his skin filthy with layers of mud, blood, excrement, and other vile things.

Sergeant Darrow called it first. "It's Monte!"

Yes . . . underneath all that shit . . . it *did* look like the poor man who had been stuffed inside a wall.

"How did he get out?" Private Rivers asked.

How indeed?

"Bring him in!" Bud shouted and was about to leap off the platform when I grabbed his arm.

"Wait," I commanded. I repeated the order loud enough for all to hear. Darrow and Private Rivers paused, ready to open the gate.

Something didn't feel right.

Something was off.

"Sir?"

Everyone waited for my decision.

"C'mon, man!" Darrow was itching to bring him inside the compound.

Had the beasts released Monte in time with the sunset?

A distraction to make us open our gates for an ambush?

But if so, where were they?

My better instincts told me not to open the door. But I could find no reason not to.

"Fine," I relented. "Let him in. Be quick!"

Bud, Darrow, and Private Rivers raced off the platforms and ran to the front door, cleared the barricade, unlocked it, and swung it open. They went out and returned quickly, supporting Monte between them.

The poor guy looked like shit shot out of a cannon.

Once Bud secured the gate, I descended from my position for a closer look, instructing Sergeant McGinley and Mister Reagan to keep watch from the platforms.

We laid Monte by the well. Darrow fetched a bucket of water while Bud began scrubbing off the grime with an old horse blanket, needing several buckets to wash away the layers of shit. By the time he finished, Monte's skin was raw. Bud paused at the crotch, and pointed.

The grime wasn't as thick there. His genitals were intact, but they were bruised to hell. The testicles had swollen to the size of navel oranges, and his pecker looked like a sad, limp little worm that had been baited on a hook and dragged around a lake. All of it looked . . . used. Something sticky and semi-clear hung off the end of his prick. I could guess what it was. What it was doing there, I hadn't a clue.

Before I could ask Bud for his thoughts, Monte suddenly rose. He looked around as if mystified by something. Somewhere a wolf howled. His good eye lit up. His cracked lips parted, he rose and howled back. Something feral overtook him. He staggered backward, throwing his arms to the sky, hands like claws searching for the moon.

Allowing Monte his moment, I addressed McGinley. Did she see anything out in the forest? I couldn't be sure the beasts weren't exploiting our distraction.

"No, nothing," she reported.

Turning to Private Rivers, I instructed him to prepare the Drummonds. They still needed to be put into position before I could ignite the calcium oxide balls and get us some light.

As we began to adjust their position, a sudden commotion on the parade ground caught my attention. Monte was scrabbling on all fours between the well and the north-facing cabin, desperately clawing at the dirt. His hands were shredded, smearing blood on the ground, yet he seemed oblivious to the pain. Darrow, attempting to intervene, stumbled after him.

Suddenly, a pained howl erupted as Darrow spun around; Monte had locked his jaw onto Darrow's wrist like a rabid dog. Blood sprayed from the wound as Darrow frantically tried to fend off his friend with his free hand.

I charged down the ramp, ordering McGinley and Private Rivers to stay with the weapons. Mister Reagan was howling with laughter near the fire pit. I shoved him aside. Stutter-heeling backward, he fell on his ass, which only made him cackle harder. Sparks flew from the fire, catching across his face.

Reaching the skirmish, I drew my pistol and used the butt to strike Monte — once, twice, three times — until he released Darrow, retreating with a hunk of flesh still clenched between his teeth. He tumbled over and scurried toward the northern cabin.

Bud rushed over with a strip of cloth. Darrow was yelping, his arm a fountain of blood. Meanwhile, Monte was digging around in the dirt, distracted by something near the tunnel door.

Good. I couldn't care less. At least he was out of our hair.

Then, I saw something that — damn it all — could have saved our lives. If only I'd known what I was looking at.

Monte twirled in the dirt, momentarily presenting his rear to me, and I could have sworn I saw a thin tail. But as quickly as it appeared, it vanished as he spun around.

*Screeeeech.*

Pulling the chain to the horizontal door, Monte revealed the tunnel below. He began to scream and jump around like a caged monkey, before looking around, finding a torch that was already burning, upright, not twenty feet from him. He ran, grabbed it, then dashed down the ramp into the tunnel.

I raced after him, my foot throbbing and on fire. I reached the tunnel, stumbled into the hole and down the ramp. He was already at the back of the tunnel, at the tangled mess of metal, torch in hand. I was pissed, in no mood for games.

"Come the fuck here." I spoke to him like the child he was. I drew my pistol — ready to shoot if he didn't comply.

He still had a crazy gleam in his eye. Smiling, he turned and faced the metal web.

Then, disturbingly, he squatted, giving me a full-moon's view of his ass.

He grunted.

The tail I thought I'd seen earlier poked out of his ass. It stretched longer as it emerged.

Only, it wasn't a tail.

A massive ball of shit dropped to the dirt. Monte squealed with joy, grabbed it, and dragged his other hand across it, wiping the shit away.

I gasped, recognizing the grenade —

As, horrifyingly, he put the twisted paper fuse in his mouth. Sucked it, cleaning it.

And raised the fuse to the torchlight.

"Oh, fuck me," I muttered.

I raised my pistol and fired.

I wasn't fast enough.

The fuse ignited as my first bullet hit him below the heart, shattering his ribs and knocking him backward. The force of the bullet made him fling the explosive behind him, where it clattered between the metal bars. Lodged somewhere inside that maze, there would be no time to retrieve it before —

I sprinted from the tunnel as it exploded, fiery dust lapping at my heels. The blast shook and swelled the ground, sending me diving for cover as debris rained down. The earth shook violently and then stilled.

When I looked up, the tunnel had collapsed into a house-sized crater. Mister Reagan, who was lolling around in the vicinity, had apparently been launched into the air, and seemed almost lucid for a moment, as he sat on his ass, stunned by the blast. Bud and Sergeant Darrow were frozen like surprised dogs, safely away from the explosion zone. On the platform, McGinley and Private Rivers wore the same expressions.

As the dust settled, I knew what was coming next.

"Turn the lights!" I screamed at McGinley and Private Rivers.

But it was too late. A cacophony of metal crashing and monstrous roars signaled the breach as the beasts surged through the hole Monte had created

Their plan became horrifyingly clear: reduce Monte to a detonating pawn to break our defenses.

I clenched my fists around my pistols, drew them, and prepared for the onslaught.

The beasts surged forth from the tunnel. Some on two legs, others on all fours, sprinting one direction or another, every which way, like spiders cut loose from an egg. I unloaded both pistols at the crowd, firing indiscriminately. I hit one, two of them in fast succession, one in the arm who kept running as if the bullet were a bug, and the other in the face. It dropped immediately.

In a lightning strike, two creatures charged the platform. I turned to see McGinley and Rivers, unable to adjust the gun or lights in time, resorting to their rifles. The first beast's head erupted into gore under their fire, and the second was clipped in the neck.

Still more creatures burst from the tunnels. We were being overrun.

And more vaulted onto the northern platform, their movements almost supernatural in their litheness. McGinley kept firing. Her aim was true, but soon her pistol went *click*. She threw it down in favor of her whip.

The leather sang through the air, slashing their faces. She whirled as if the whip were an extension of her being. Her primal screams seemed to instill a deep fear in the beasts, who hesitated at the edge of her reach. Lashing one across the snout, she used the momentum to wrap the whip around another's neck. Its eyes bulged in shock as it clawed at the constricting leather. With a Herculean effort, McGinley yanked, sending the creature tumbling from the platform.

I shouted in triumph, but the moment was fleeting. The beast's weight pulled her off balance. She fell from the platform, landing on her back with a sick thud. Her breath sputtered in her throat as she gasped for air.

"No!" I sprinted toward her, firing relentlessly at the encroaching horde.

It was too late.

She was swallowed by the mass of bodies, and the last I saw was her severed head tossed skyward by a grotesque claw.

Apparently, she was not what they wanted.

I dodged the grasp of a smashed-snouted humanoid, its chest marred with long rivers of twisting scars. The creature shrieked hideously and stiffened before collapsing from my next bullet.

I looked to the platform — *the lights*! I could still ignite the calcium oxide and drive them away.

I sidestepped an errant claw and kept running. A crash to the west drew my gaze just in time to see one smash the first light with a rock. It then hurled the Drummond off the platform, where it landed mangled and useless. The creature, silhouetted against the moonlight, raised its arms with a victorious roar. From my vantage point looking up, I saw what can only be described as doom incarnate.

I had not made it halfway to the platforms when the second light crashed down, and both Gatling guns toppled. Private Rivers, attempting to reload, was struck by a massive clawed hand. He teetered off the platform with the weapon's dead weight and fell with a thud onto his back.

They took him.

I fired the last of my bullets, turning to see Bud, his face a mask of terror as a humanoid sunk its claws into his side. It tightened, drawing blood. Bud screamed as he was dragged into the darkness, and then I heard no more.

As for Sergeant Darrow and Mister Reagan, they gave little fight. Reagan, due to his deteriorated mental state, hadn't even drawn a weapon. Instead, he'd simply sat in the parade ground. Cross-legged, he waited patiently to be taken.

Darrow, however, had emptied his pistols in futile panic. I glimpsed a creature stepping heavily on his back, driving him face-first into the dirt. His shouts muffled, he ceased struggling, conserving his breath in the dust.

Just like that, the battle was over.

# CHAPTER 16

Fighting was pointless, I knew that much.

Claws shredded my clothes and pinned me to the dirt. I shivered, but not from the cold. A blindfold was pulled roughly over my eyes.

They flipped me over, wrapping me in a skin-tight cocoon of cloth, pinning my arms across my chest. Then they rolled me onto my side, securing the binding — I couldn't tell if it was stitched, knotted, or clasped. Suddenly I was flung over a shoulder, the bone striking me in the stomach and knocking my breath away.

Next thing I knew, I was being run through the forest at high speed. The silence of my captors unnerved me; there was no panting, no signs of fatigue. It became clear to me then that we could never have escaped the outpost on our own. Our suspicions were accurate: the escapees had been allowed to leave.

As we leaped through the air, I felt a momentary weightlessness before crashing back to the earth, my ribs cracking from the impact. Thankfully, I could still scream — it was a sign I was still alive.

My blindfold shifted, allowing me a sliver of sight. I glimpsed the ground rushing beneath us. Feet thundered. In the tepid moonlight, they were big and ghastly, with a claw jutting from the outer edge of each. Once again, I was peering down a twisting and tortuous ladder of evolution. The voids of time contain some things worse than nothing.

I felt another bout of weightlessness, only this time it didn't end. Gravity had merely shifted, tilting me backward, and suddenly I was staring not at the ground but at the inverted wall of the mine. Counting quickly, I discerned there were four others being carried alongside me — Bud, Rivers, even the bastards Darrow and Mister Reagan, were alive.

The ground leveled out, and soon it didn't matter that my blindfold had slipped because it was much too dark to see anyway. The thing carrying me hunched over and accelerated through the tunnel at an impossible speed.

The passageways twisted and turned, disorienting me completely. I lost track of trying to count left and right turns as waves of nausea overwhelmed me; any hope of mapping our route vanished as we delved deeper into the bowels of the mountain.

Just as I felt vomit rising in my throat, the humanoid halted and loosened its grip around my waist. The sound of creaking wood — a door opening, perhaps. We took a few more steps, and the air grew damper and heavier. We were in a new room.

Dear God.

Unceremoniously, I was dumped onto a rocky floor. My chest slammed against the hard surface, knocking the wind out of me. Around me, I could hear the thuds of others being dropped, their gasps and groans filling the room.

The sound of the wooden door creaking shut sealed our fate, confining us in a makeshift cell somewhere within the earth.


Days passed.

Or, perhaps, hours that felt like days. Who could tell? In the pitch black, wrapped up as I was in the mummy-tight cloth, time moved strangely. All I knew is that twice I had to relieve myself, and was presently soaking in my own waste.

We were afraid to speak.

How could we know if they were nearby, watching, waiting to punish us?

But after a time, I braved the unknown to whisper. I needed an account of who was there, who was injured, who, if anyone, had died in the interim. From what I could tell, Bud was immediately to my left, and going clockwise, Private Rivers followed. No one was directly across from me; it seemed I was placed against the back wall opposite the entrance. To my right were Mister Reagan and Sergeant Darrow, the latter muttering curses under his breath, too caught up in his own misery to engage with me. Mister Reagan was, again, eerily silent.

They offered only grunts in response, likely because their mouths were covered. For whatever reason, Darrow and I were spared this indignity.

Then —

A bit of light, a faint sliver of yellow and gold.

I shook my head. I must have been imagining things.

But, no. It was real.

The light was slowly advancing toward us.

Bud saw it, too. He whimpered at this miraculous vision. The humanoid carrying it emerged from around a corner. The source wasn't a torch but a kerosene lamp, its glass chimney coated in dirt, which muted its glow.

Despite the relief at seeing light, I couldn't help but wonder why they would bring it, considering their aversion to brightness.

Then the grim realization dawned on me.

They wanted us to see.

*But why?*

The humanoid approached. Its face appeared crushed by some immense weight, with deep, overlapping folds of skin. The eyes, just visible through tiny slits, gave it a grotesque appearance. This one was markedly older, with a severely hunched back, and moved with deliberate slowness. Our grim jailer.

"Anyone got a knife?" I whispered as the creature drew nearer. I glanced at Mister Reagan, now visible in the faint light, but he was unreachable.

The jailer, Folded-Face, paused about ten feet from our cell. Another beast, taller and seemingly younger, joined him. Grunts and whispers resonated off the stony walls. They were yammering about something.

Two more creatures emerged from the shadows. It was a menacing assembly. One had arms twice the length of the others; I figured it could have been a result of some birth defect. The fourth, however, had the unmistakable bearing of a warrior: lean, muscular, brutish.

A council formed. We held our breath; a preternatural feeling told us silence might keep us safe.

This proved an illusion.

Warrior and Folded-Face stepped forward and slid open the wooden cell door made of vertical bars. They looked like specters from a nightmarish vision, their claws clacking ominously on the stone floor. Long Arms lingered just outside the cell, and what he was doing I couldn't believe at first. I had to glance twice to make sure it was real.

He was fondling his disturbingly large penis, breathing heavily as he did so. I turned away. It was too much to watch.

Warrior scanned our group, momentarily locking eyes with each of us. I tried to remain invisible.

His attention finally settled on Sergeant Darrow, and stepped decisively towards him. At this, Long Arms issued a sharp bark, prompting the warrior to glance back for confirmation.

I remembered clearly then. This Long Arms was the one who had taken a unsettling interest in him back at the cave.

Darrow recognized this, too. He whimpered, begged to be left alone, but it was no use. Warrior wrapped a claw around his head, dragging him out of the cell like a child's doll. No amount of squirming or screaming would help him now.

Warrior flung the poor bastard down. Wraps were torn off and discarded. Folded-Face quickly secured Darrow's legs with a rope, threw the other end over a protruding rock, and pulled it tight, lifting him with ease until he was suspended upside down.

Then they ripped off his pants, leaving him exposed; his shirt slid over his face.

Long Arms, meanwhile, continued his obscenities, his grotesque member now fully engorged, well over a foot in length, swinging ominously as he approached. With deliberate movements, he spread Darrow's legs wide. Folded-Face joined him, and together they probed and prodded at Darrow's genitals, muttering to each other in a series of grunts and clicks that sounded like a sinister consultation.

They seemed to reach a decision, and signaled to Warrior, who adjusted the rope, allowing Darrow's head to thump dully against the rocky floor.

Long Arms, now kneeling, brought his face disturbingly close to Darrow's dick before putting the measly thing in his mouth. Darrow's reaction was immediate and visceral — he writhed and screamed, his legs flailing as he experienced the horrifying sensation of a rough, slimy tongue against his skin.

The creatures paid no mind to Darrow's outburst. If anything, they encouraged it.

Long Arms worked on Darrow's prick for a minute or so. The sodomy was nothing short of revolting. The sight was too much for me. I spewed vomit down my front.

I forced my eyes shut, hoping to block out the horror, but the images were already seared into my mind. When I dared to look again, Long Arms had stepped back, leaving Darrow in a state of distressing arousal.

The act that followed was even more grotesque and disturbing.

Long Arms reached down and lifted his own python, exposing a gash beneath it. Positioning Darrow appropriately, he forcefully inserted Darrow's erect member into his slit, in a perverted mimicry of copulation. Long Arms manipulated his own body with disturbing fervor, thrusting against Darrow's inverted form, his arms encircling Darrow's ass.

The act was hideous beyond words, a nightmarish tableau of violation and depravity.

When it was over, Long Arms pushed the silent soldier aside and laid down on his back with his legs in the air. Folded-Face muttered something to Long Arms, who answered him but refused to move.

Folded-Face seemed to think a moment.

Then he lifted a claw and slashed Darrow's throat.

Darrow made no sound as the blood gurgled from his neck and streamed down his body, painting his front red in an instant. Arterial spray almost reached us in the cell, then died as the pressure dissipated.

Folded-Face dug a long claw into Darrow's soft belly, disemboweling him. Innards spilled and piled on the ground, his liver sliding down and resting on top of the pile.

I kept my eyes shut until I heard them remove Darrow. My body felt drained, numb. Tears, dried on my cheeks, were replaced by more. I had no strength left, physically or mentally.

When they lifted me, I almost welcomed it. It signified less time until death. A swift end was all I could hope for.

Abruptly, I was flung to the ground as my bindings were torn away, leaving my skin raw. My hands were swiftly tied, and I was suspended like the other before me.

Confronting Warrior directly, I recoiled from the hot, fetid breath streaming from its gaping mouth. My shirt was ripped away. The dim glow of the kerosene lamp cast a monstrous light, revealing a network of veins that marred its snout like the flushed face of a chronic drinker.

I screamed as it tore off my pants. The damp air enveloped my testicles, and I felt a claw flick across my penis. It was an invasive, mocking touch. My genitals, shrunken in terror, tried to retreat into my body. But there was no escape.

It seemed it was now Warrior's turn for depravity, his grip encircling my genitals with a painful squeeze. Every attempt to kick only intensified the pain, a deep, sickening ache spreading across my abdomen.

I clenched my eyes shut, bracing for the worst.

But then, the grip loosened.

I risked opening an eye. The ruddy-faced humanoid was now arguing with a newcomer. The tension escalated quickly; they barked and gestured wildly at each other.

Suddenly, the second humanoid shoved the other aside and lunged at me, freeing me from my bindings. In a flash, I was hoisted over its shoulder and whisked away. As we left the chamber, Warrior's frustrated roars faded behind us, the reverberations of his fury vanishing as we rounded the corner.

I had no time to think, to plan an escape. Just moments after leaving the room, I saw where I was being taken.

My scream got stuck in my throat.

No!

Desperation took over, and I thrashed violently, clawing at the creature's back, pounding it with my fists. It barely registered my attacks.

We approached the small, dismal cell built into the wall, its entrance barred by a wood door. Another creature was already there, opening it for us.

I struggled, but my strength was ebbing. The beast hurled me into the cell headfirst with such force that I skidded across the floor of the confined space. I tried to turn and orient myself, but the cell was too narrow, wide enough for my body but not by much, and only a few feet tall.

After thrusting a water bucket inside, they locked the cell. The bars creaked ominously as they secured them, sealing me in this tiny, muddy prison. In a panic, I scrambled to turn around, thinking if I could just face the other way, I might find a way out.

I pushed against the left wall, trying in vain to swing my legs around to the right. But the space was too tight.

Eventually, common sense prevailed, and I bent my knees, contorting my body to find enough room to turn.

"No! Goddamnit, you sons of bitches!"

But they were already gone.

Silence settled in, oppressive and complete.

I strained to hear anything. No sound of water dripping, no footsteps — nothing.

Trapped, I faced the horrifying possibility of being forgotten here, left to die slowly in this claustrophobic hell.

I was determined to maintain my sanity, to resist the madness that had claimed the others. But that resolve was short-lived; I knew this blackness would swallow me whole. I would not escape it, just as I could not escape the darkness that had haunted me most every night since I left home eighteen years before. Until now, I always had the light of a fire to comfort me. But here I would be engulfed. For good this time.

In the silence that enveloped me, I heard a voice. Real or imagined, it didn't matter. Its tone was both mocking and final.

"Goodnight," it whispered.

# CHAPTER 17

The mind is a marvelous thing. Deprived of stimuli, it conjures dreams, memories, hallucinations without any help from its owner. It keeps working under any circumstances. As time passed, my mind took me far away from the blank void that had become my home. I didn't try to stop it — I couldn't.

Time turned into an endless nothing. An entire world was constructed within the confines of my brain. Sometimes, I would wake from these dreams to face a new wave of terror. During these moments, I took care of basic needs; I relieved myself, drank the brackish water left for me. The harsh reality of my situation, too overwhelming to bear, would eventually recede, and once more I would find myself on battlefields, distant prairies, or at home . . . with Angie.

Ah, Angie.

Visions of her were all that kept me going. She was my tether, my rope to sanity. I gave myself to those hallucinations, and gladly. I wondered if she was still waiting for me. She had to be. I had no choice but to believe.

And time passed.

At first, I thought the opening of the cell door was a dream, too. Actually, I hoped it was. I had grown comfortable in my delusion. Why leave?

But reality came for me regardless, its claws dragging me from my tomb. Strangely, I felt no panic, no anxiety; my heart neither skipped a beat nor pounded with fear.

Two creatures were carrying me, one gripping my shoulders, the other securing my legs. To them, I must have seemed as light as a gerbil, or perhaps a small poodle cradled by those elegantly coiffed ladies in New York. I offered no resistance. Perhaps I had crossed the Rubicon into the afterlife, or maybe I was approaching Saint Peter. At that moment, the destination seemed irrelevant — I was merely a passenger, carried onward by forces beyond my control.

A sense of peace washed over me, and then —


Were my eyes open?

A faint glimmer cleaved the darkness as a match sparked to life. A candle was lit. As the feeble flame struggled against the gloom, a form began to emerge from the haze. There, illuminated gradually by the growing light, was a figure with human hair. It had no snout.

It lit another candle, and then another. Each new flame brought me back more and more.

I tried to sit up, but my legs, weakened and atrophied from prolonged confinement in the rock cage, failed me. I collapsed back onto what felt like a raised wooden plank — a bed? Instinctively, my hand darted to my side searching for my pistol, but in its place, I found only the rough texture of a hide loincloth wrapped around my waist.

The figure leaned forward into the yellow light. My vision was clarified. It extended a hand. It held cooked meat. I snatched it, swallowed it without chewing. Venison. It dripped. When I finished, I sucked my filthy fingers and hands dry.

Jacob simply watched.

Wavy brown hair fell across his forehead like a comma. Sun-scorched skin gave his face character beyond his eighteen years. Soft bits of patchy beard illustrated his jaw and chin and neck. His ears were scrunched and shrunken, jutting out from his skull at haphazard angles. His eyes were beady and dark, the right one turned slightly inward. The left eye sat higher than the right, adding to his hopelessly lopsided appearance. His lips were thin, cracked, and white. His mouth resembled an inverted V.

His appearance was so markedly uneven, so unbalanced, that I could hardly look at him.

"It's really you." Jacob's words fell from his mouth, harsh and grumbling. He struggled to form them properly. He pulled the candle closer to his face, so he was lit from below, emphasizing his freakish, preternatural look. "Nathaniel."

I tried to speak. The barren desert of my mouth prevented it. I looked away, unable to bear the green snot — *or was it pus?* — that gathered between his nose and mouth.

He moved to his left, intercepting my gaze. Drew closer to me, making it harder for me to turn away. My heartbeat quickened. I scurried backward, shrank against the wall behind me. His face loomed, distorted. He sensed my horror. I saw something like disappointment on his face, insofar as I could see anything resembling humanity on him.

He retreated and sat down, watching me with a sideways gaze. Graciously, he had turned to the wall, sparing me a grisly view.

"Christ," he said, "I won't bite." He wiped his nose, stuff dripping from his fingers, which he then smeared on his loincloth, already marked with nauseating streaks of green and yellow.

I began to retch.

"You ate too fast," he observed as I finished up. His speech was uniquely disrupted, likely from the great quantities of mucus he produced that also seemed to cause him shortness of breath.

He rose and lit a couple more candles around the room, bringing the space into greater focus. There were no windows, of course, and the ceiling was low enough that his head touched it when he stood up. Wooden benches lined the opposite side of the room, and a bookshelf with nothing on it was propped against the wall.

"The war," he said abruptly. "Who's winning?"

My throat felt like a feline's scratching post. "War?"

"Union. Confederacy."

"The war's been over a year. The Union won."

"Union?" Jacob sounded surprised. "Thank God for that." With his shrunken, malformed right hand — the same one I remembered from the crib years ago — he made the sign of the cross. Then, lowering his head into his open palm, he exposed the crown of his misshapen skull. The bones had never formed properly, giving it a pointed appearance. His scalp was covered in scaly, crusty skin, with a spotty coverage of rough, hairy patches. Absently, he picked at the dry skin. A nervous habit, perhaps.

I spoke, steadying myself. "What's happening here?"

He pondered the bits of skin between his fingers, which fluttered to the floor like dry leaves.

"Am I a prisoner? Are *you*?"

Something bumped against the plank of wood that leaned against the roughly hewn door frame. My heart skipped a beat at the thought of who might come in.

"Don't worry," he said. "I told 'em not to come in. We need privacy. They won't hurt you anyway. Not now. You're with me."

I struggled to speak. I mumbled something about the beasts letting me leave. How could we escape?

"Escape?" He caught my eye.

"Help me get out. Please."

"Help you?" A hurt look crossed Jacob's face as if my words had wounded him deeply. "You didn't come for me?" He seemed to wrestle with a complex thought. "I thought you did. Because . . ."

"Because what?"

"Because we're kin." His eyes looked glassy, vacant.

My mouth quivered. I could barely croak. "Brothers. Yes."

He looked sideways at me, scrutinizing, as if to catch me in a lie. Then his eyes lit up. He suddenly seemed wild, a feral thing. Volatile. Something human but perhaps not quite; God had made an uncanny thing. "Tell me," he said. "Tell me — who you reckon we are to each other."

A rock blocked my throat.

"Brothers."

"No!" He pounded his fist against the cracked wooden crate to his right. "Spit it out. The whole truth. Or I'll have 'em pound you. And your men."

The candle flame hissed. I glanced back and forth, from Jacob to the ground, and shifted in my chair.

*A hand crests the length of the cool sheet above my back, then pulls it aside, exposing the small of my back.*

"I know the truth. You tell me now."

*"Don't wake," she whispers. "I'm not really here."*

I shook my head. Squeezed my eyes shut.

No.

*NO.*

"Yes."

I smelled something rank. Jacob leaned in close. I felt him grasp my hands as he sank to his knees. I opened my eyes. He put his head in my lap.

No.

"Why'd you run away from me?"

*God, please forgive me.*

"Why'd you try to kill me?"

*I retreat somewhere inside myself. I feel her hands on my body . . .*

"You 'barrassed? Of me?" he said.

*. . . down there.*

I looked at Jacob's misshapen head. I saw him then, and in the crib, as if the eighteen years apart had been hollowed out and our moments together compressed into one.

My brother?

Yes.

And no.

"You're my father," he said.

I could feel his disfigured, grotesque bone structure digging uncomfortably into my thigh. But I did not recoil.

Instead, I placed a trembling hand on the back of his head. The tears fell then. I did not stop them.

"Yes." I croaked. "Your father. *And* your brother."

# CHAPTER 18

As autumn approached, Father prepared to leave for the apple farms to the east. The year had been tough; little had grown nearby, compelling him to find work in more distant regions. He and James Merriman loaded up the wagon while I stood beside Mother, watching them depart, waving them goodbye.

Father and Mother were getting on in years, and they were anxious to have another child before it was too late. But nothing seemed to work. Mother began bringing home strange herbs. Nurses visited. I even heard whispers that they had visited a conjure man. They were desperate.

Their struggle left Father disturbed. He felt like less of a man.

She started visiting me the night he left.

I wanted to fight her off. Of course I did.

At first, I tried.

But what's a boy to do?

The fact is, my mind froze when she touched me. Kissed me. And more. I simply couldn't think, couldn't say a word.

And to my shame, my body . . . responded to her advances.

Why me?

Why did she choose me?

Why not another man in town?

*Why?*


As time passed, Mother's visits became less frequent, and, when she got what she wanted, they stopped altogether. Her interest in me waned; our conversations dwindled to almost nothing. Left on my own, I found solace spending time with Angie and dedicating myself to the barn and the animals.

When Father finally returned, my joy at seeing him was overwhelming. I rushed to him, my embrace fierce enough to nearly rip the fabric of his jacket.

I said nothing about what had happened between me and Mother. What *could* I tell him?

Life went on.

Until one day I was milking the cow in the barn. A silhouette crossed the light. I turned. There was Father, his hat in his hands. He told me to follow him.

We went into the kitchen and I sat down. Mother retreated upstairs. I could hear her footsteps fade away, and we were alone. Father wiped his brow and hung his hat by the door.

"I want you to tell me the truth now," he said, stabbing a shaky finger at me. "You lie to me, I'm gonna whoop you."

I told him yes, sir. He rose, went to his little hiding spot behind the false door in the cupboard, and poured himself a whiskey from a stashed bottle. He looked stricken. His face was white. I couldn't imagine what he was going to say. He sat down, leaning heavily on the table.

"When I left for work," he said, "Did another man come to the house?"

"Another man?"

"Jackson Shepard? Martin Brooks, maybe?"

I shook my head.

"You're sure?"

"I saw no one. It was just me and Mother."

"She ever leave the house? More than a few hours?" He pressed further, his eyes searching mine for something I didn't understand.

I thought hard. But nothing came to mind; my memories were clear. "I don't know."

A fuse was lit inside him. His face hardened. "Think," he urged. His hands gripped the edge of the wooden table, knuckles turning white.

"I — I don't think so."

Father peered darkly at me. His eyes were cloudy, intense. Something doomed sprouted behind them. He seemed a different man than the one who'd left months before.

Then, with an abruptness that startled me, he stood and walked to the counter. His shoulders slumped as he leaned one hand against the windowsill; the other tightly clutched the glass of bourbon. It threatened to shatter in his grip. He looked so old.

"Your mother is pregnant again." He swallowed what was left in his glass and stared into the bottom of it. "Doc says she's a few months along." He turned to me. "A few months. Right in the middle of when I was gone, son. Smack dab in the goddamn middle."

He set his drink down with a definitive clink and walked out. The door closed with a soft thud behind him. I watched through the window, frozen in place at the kitchen table, as he disappeared into the fading light. I wanted to go outside, to comfort him, to say something — anything, but . . .

I stayed in the kitchen, the silence growing heavier as the shadows lengthened and the room darkened into evening.

Then —

The gunshot came.

I charged outside and ran to the barn. I found him propped against the wall, surrounded by hay. Light streamed through the barn door, illuminating half his face. The darker side, along with most of his jaw, had been blown away. He was still alive but gagging on his own blood. The rifle lay against the ground beside him. He'd used his toe to pull the trigger. It seemed he had flinched at the last moment — perhaps a moment of doubt or a change of heart.

He tried to speak, but only produced garbled sounds. I fell to my knees beside him, reaching out to help, but as I touched him, part of his shattered skull fell away, mixing bits of brain and bone with the hay.

Kneeling in the blood-soaked straw, I found a cold comfort knowing he had never discovered the truth.

After his funeral, I kept my distance from Mother. As her pregnancy advanced, my resentment towards what was growing inside her deepened. I went to school, but even there, I was isolated, shunned by the other children as if the despair that had driven my father to end his life was contagious.

The secret between me and Mother gnawed at me, yet I confided in no one. I tried to convince myself it didn't matter. The truth needn't be shared; in any case, who would I have told? Occasionally, I managed to persuade myself that it was all just a terrible nightmare — that none of this could possibly be real. Such tragedies only happened to other people.

Meanwhile, Mother thrived on my discomfort, often with a sly smirk that suggested she found some perverse pleasure in my distress. She moved about her daily routines with an eerie self-sufficiency. We coexisted like strangers under the same roof.

Eventually, something inside me just broke. I couldn't face it—what I had done, what had been done to me. What it would mean if you came into this world. How could I live with all of us under the same roof? Would she laugh at me forever?

When I looked at you, would all I see be a constant reminder of her evil?

Would you turn out to become like her?

I couldn't fathom any of it. It was too much. Too much for a fourteen-year-old boy to handle.

So, when Mother's labor ended and you were born, and when Doctor Leclaire insisted I look into your crib, I knew I had to end it.

# CHAPTER 19

I finished my story, my gaze anchored to the floor as the words died. When my eyes finally met Jacob's, he was softly crying. His face, so peculiar and unnerving, was streaked with tears that mingled with the green snot. He looked odd, almost extraterrestrial. Despite my revulsion, something else welled up within me. Pity, guilt, shame, love — I still struggle to name it.

I reached out, gently placing my hand on Jacob's shoulder. I hesitated to pull him into a full embrace. His skin was feverishly warm.

Suddenly, Jacob surged toward me, abandoning any attempt to restrain himself. He wept openly, throwing his arms around me, seeking solace from his father and brother.

My lower lip trembled. A profound ache burgeoned within my chest, an overwhelming sensation that threatened to consume me. A shift began to occur, deep inside me. His hug, his caress . . . something was transmitted in them. It was as if I finally felt him — my brother, my son. It took an actual embrace to know he was indeed real. I'd never touched him as a child — this was our first contact. It felt as if I'd been running from an abstraction for more than half my life. He wasn't real before, and then he was.

I could pull away from him, try to run, but I found that I didn't want to.

I wanted to stay.

I felt pity, loathing, revulsion, all those things, yes; but beneath them I felt something else, too.

He was deformed, disgusting even, but he was human. A real man. Not like these creatures in the cave. It wasn't his fault he was born this way, any more than it is anyone's fault for being born at all.

Eighteen years ago, I was mistaken. I was selfish. I'd tried to rid myself of him, to kill him.

I gasped in realization. I'd left him alone, with Mother . . .

How could I have left him with her?

I hugged him tighter. The tears came. I didn't stop them.

What had she done to him while I was gone? What kinds of torture had she subjected him to? The thought was unbearable.

In my haste to leave, to kill him and go, I'd forgotten, or never realized, who the real monster was in all this. It wasn't me. And it wasn't Jacob.

It was her.

Mother.

She was the bad one.

We were both victims, I knew then. He and I both. Mother had violated our family.

He shook in my arms, and I in his. The rock in my chest began to move, to dislodge itself with the torrent of our tears.

I was not to blame, but it was my responsibility to make things right.

We remained locked in our embrace. A bond was created then, and affirmed.

My son. My brother.

We were linked, not just by blood, but by something else altogether.

Gravity, you see?


I followed Jacob through the labyrinthine hallways, feeling as though I were trapped in some bizarre and illogical nightmare. I had no idea which direction we were headed; I had asked him to take me to my surviving men, but he simply waved a dismissive hand, suggesting "in time."

He had something else to show me.

We'd remained in our embrace, sobbing with each other, for what I estimate to be the better part of an hour. Now I trailed behind him, our route meandering right and left, wondering just how deep into the mountain we were going. These hallways were far larger than the typical mining tunnels; it seemed that over the centuries, the humanoids had perfected their construction, optimizing the dimensions and airflow to prevent suffocation. Occasionally, I felt what seemed like a breeze — an impossible occurrence in such a place. Yet, there it was.

The creatures we encountered along the way didn't dare to impede us. Instead, they scurried away or pressed themselves flat against the walls, some even bowing their heads in deference as we passed.

Why? What role did Jacob play among them?

Their pungent odor cocooned me, and twice I stopped to gag — the fetid, rotten cheese stench of gangrene was too much to bear.

Finally, Jacob halted and turned into a room, holding the door open for me. Inside, a figure on a makeshift bed caught my eye.

The humanoid woman lying there had long hair and soft facial features that sharply contrasted with her more beast-like traits: a pronounced snout framed by high cheekbones.

As she shifted, her gaze fell on us, her hand protectively covering her belly.

Jacob knelt beside her, his hand gently covering hers. He smiled at me. "You're gonna be an uncle — and a grandfather."

My knees buckled.

"This is Lilith," Jacob explained, sensing my shock. "I named her after Ma." He tenderly stroked her hair.

Jacob had mated with one of them?

How?

Were they somehow human, after all, or had Bud and I overlooked something in our analysis?

He saw the confusion written on my face. Standing, he took the lantern to the wall, illuminating some pictographs that had been drawn there long ago.

"Their bloodline went bad," Jacob said. "Ain't been a young one birthed here in a good many years." His fingers traced the pictures. "How they tell it, way back when, they got forced down under the dirt, and they took to breeding with themselves.

"It stopped working. No more births, see?" He glanced at his lady. "They're a dying breed."

I pieced it together. Bud's instinct about their mutilations . . .

"So that's why they've been taking our troops? To mate with them?"

He nodded. "Tryin' to. Only none of them sprouted. Until I came along." He said it with pride. "I grew up thinking my defects was a curse. I knew my own brother tried to murder me in my crib. Whole town knew so. Thought I was some kinda freak out of a carnival. Even pondered joining one. What kinda other life could I have, lookin' like this?

"But Price, he gave me the job, to come here. Once Ma died, there was no point in staying. Got took prisoner just like all them others we come here with. But I had something the others didn't. To them, I'm a savior. Whatever's inside me is workin'. Whatever changes got brought out 'cause of my birth is helping. Helping them. I'm the first to give one of 'em a child in a long time."

He looked at me with grateful tears in his eyes. "And it's all 'cause of you."

"Me?"

He nodded. "'Cause you made me different. 'Cause you and Ma did what you did. Something went wrong with my birth. Inbreeding. But it's okay — I match 'em! It's helping 'em survive!"

He caressed his wife's glistening belly. "And this is gonna be your grandson. It's a miracle."

"It's . . . inhuman," I whispered.

"They got as much a right to live as you, don't they? The Lord chose me to help 'em. He chose you, too. You think you know better than the Lord?"

I couldn't wrap myself around it. It was too much. I shook my head.

Jacob was not pleased.

"Don't you get it? Out there, I was nothin'. Alone, seekin' my pa, a friend. The schoolboys tormented me for my looks till I was less'n dirt.

"And then I come here, to this place. And I see these . . . creatures. They're kin to me. Who'd of thought I'd find my true calling here?"

He knelt beside his wife. She greeted him with a lopsided smile, her head gleaming as if coated in duck fat. Suddenly, her expression twisted in pain; she grimaced, clutching her swollen belly. It was massive, veined vividly in contrast to her gray-green, stone-like skin.

"You'd want me to leave, to abandon my child?" He looked up at me. "Abandon my wife?" His jaw set. "Like you did to me? You gonna run out on us again? Leave your family? Me, her, this youngster? Look what you created. You don't have pride about that?"

The massive belly on the bed rumbled. The thing he called Lilith moaned.

"Something good finally comes from what Ma did to us. And you wanna run? This is a miracle. You don't run from God's miracles."

*You don't run from God's miracles.*

What, I thought, is the opposite of a miracle?

Not an hour before I had accepted Jacob as my brother, my son. Now I was asked to accept the fact that the inbreeding that produced Jacob was now the key to the survival of this entire race. That I was going to be a grandfather to one of these things.

These creatures had been stranded on an ambiguous rung of the evolutionary ladder — yet somehow, nature had carved a path forward.

Through Jacob.

Through me.

A voice inside me spoke. I argued with myself.

*But these creatures are horrid. They're evil.*

Why? Because they fight to survive? Because they kill? So do we.

*It's unnatural!*

How could anything natural be unnatural? What if this new lineage, birthed from Jacob and his mate, marked the emergence of a new species? Wasn't that a marvel, a cause for celebration?

How was it anything but the work of an omnipotent, omniscient God?

Engrossed in these thoughts, I was abruptly jolted back to the present by a piercing scream. Jacob was already springing into action, lifting his wife from the soiled bed where a viscous substance leaked.

"It's time," he said, urgency in his voice as he carried her out of the room.

Dear God, I thought.

It's happening.

The birth.

# CHAPTER 20

In a cavernous chamber, lit by the flames of a bonfire, Lilith labored to bring new life into the world. She lay on her back upon a stone slab elevated a few feet off the ground, Jacob kneeling next to her. A natural chimney in the rock ceiling let the thick smoke escape. Surrounding us, massive stone pillars rose from the ground, stretching toward the distant ceiling, framing the primordial birthing ceremony.

Dozens, maybe a hundred, of the barbarians crowded around, witnessing the first birth of their kind in many years. Their eyes shone wide and gleaming in the firelight as they murmured amongst themselves in their strange language, a symphony of clicks like stones clacking.

I watched them. Positioned behind one of the pillars, I kept a safe distance from the heat of the bonfire and the intensity of the impending birth. I felt their constant gaze upon me, too, yet they maintained a distance. It seemed some command had been issued, for they accorded me a deference similar to that shown to Jacob.

After all, I was the grandfather.

I had to marvel at these beings. Filthy, yes. Nauseating, yes. Odious and revolting and detestable and . . . pitiful. The more time I spent among them, the clearer their frailty became. Many suffered from the same affliction of green mucus as Jacob, and frequently, without warning, they would double over in spasmodic coughing fits, spattering blood upon the ground. On our way in, in fact, we'd passed a sick room in which over a dozen of the things were huddled in corners or laid out on stone beds. Looked like consumption patients, with their withered limbs and hollow, sunken faces.

The birth was imminent; Lilith labored heavily, panting and sweating with Jacob steadfast by her side. Around the stone altar, creatures had gathered closely, bowing their heads in their lengthy fingers. I suppose even fiends must pray at times. Others remained at the outskirts of the space, wary and standoffish.

I needed a plan. My soldiers were either dead or being held captive, and I had no clue where they might be. As I tried to orient myself within the cavern, the sound of a chain rattling nearby drew my attention.

Mister Reagan was standing next to me, stark naked. A metal ring encircled his neck, from which the chain extended, held by one of the creatures at the other end. His expression was the same as before: he had none.

With a grunt and a rattle of the chain, the beast signaled, and Mister Reagan, compliant, walked to the center of the room. There, his captor forced him to his knees beside Jacob and Lilith.

A hush fell over the chamber. The murmurs quieted, and the sound of claws clicking against the stone floor ceased. The only noises that remained were the crackling of the fire and Lilith's labored moans. The creatures had packed in tightly around me, each one jostling for a view of the impending birth, leaving me hemmed in, shoulder to shoulder with them.

Catching sight of me, Jacob issued a command. The crowd parted, allowing me passage. Soon, I found myself kneeling near my brother-son, surrounded by an intense and expectant silence.

Mister Reagan, lost in himself, stared blankly into the fire, oblivious to my presence.

Three of the humanoids approached him from behind. With a surprising gentleness, they half-carried him to the base of Lilith's feet, where a small area had been cleared for him. There, they laid him down and began to wrap him in their peculiar cloth, their claws moving with swift and precise efficiency. In just a few moments, Mister Reagan was swaddled from head to toe.

Just before the cloth covered his face, his eyes met mine. The intensity in his gaze was so piercing that it overwhelmed me, compelling me to look away. Yet I could sense that his stare remained fixed on me, unbroken and penetrating, even as they shielded his eyes.

The tallest of the creatures produced a blade. In one quick, unforgiving motion, he slit Mister Reagan's throat. Dark blood spilled over Lilith's lower half. As Mister Reagan convulsed, the humanoid positioned his head so the blood from his wound flowed directly onto Lilith's sex. His convulsions slowed to twitches, then ceased altogether.

The flow trickled and stopped. The viscous blood obscured Lilith's genitals. Unceremoniously, the tallest one tossed Mister Reagan's body into the fire. The flesh hissed and burned, emitting a foul smell. The humanoids around me erupted into cheers.

It was time.

Jacob assumed his place at the end of the stone slab between Lilith's widely splayed legs, making sure she was fully exposed for the birth. He leaned in close, whispering words that seemed to coax and comfort her. His words were lost to me, drowned out by the sickening sizzle of Mister Reagan's flesh as it burned on the fire. The humanoids around us became restless, their excitement palpable in the charged air. They shuffled and murmured among themselves, their anticipation for the impending birth growing.

Lilith pushed.

Jacob's deformed hand caressed her swollen belly, guiding the life within.

Human births may come slowly, but this one did not. The moment arrived with primal intensity.

A visceral cry from deep within Lilith accompanied her final push.

Amidst the thick air and the stifling anticipation, a new sound pierced the cavern. It was a sharp, startling wail, robust and full of life.

The baby declared its arrival.

Jacob lifted the child. It was slick with blood and feces. But it was alive! Lilith reached for it; I saw in her eyes a maternal — and humanlike — love. She brushed her fingers against the tiny, damp head and body. Looking around, I noticed others weeping. Perhaps they were more like us than I realized.

Then, the mood shifted palpably. A hush swept through the crowd, followed by whispers that rippled like disturbed water. Something confused them. Everyone pressed closer, eager yet apprehensive to see the newborn.

I craned forward to see.

The baby had —

No elongated snout.

No oversized teeth.

No clawed feet.

Instead, little hands. Short, stubby legs. A head.

The inbred male and humanoid female had given birth to a . . .

Human?

The creatures surrounding us fell silent.

Fear and disgust rippled through the crowd as the realization set in: the child they had awaited was not of their own kind. This was not the progeny they had envisioned; this was something else entirely.

Warrior forced his way through. The chatter of the crowd hushed once more. All eyes were drawn to him. He loomed over the scene, casting his gaze down upon the newborn in Lilith's arms and carefully examining the umbilical cord.

Lilith hissed. Steadying her with a hand, Jacob stood and faced Warrior. He grunted something. In response, Warrior turned to the others. He gestured at the child, chirping, grunting, and clicking. My skin tingled. The hordes murmured.

A cry cut through the noise, stark and alarming. It was swiftly repeated and amplified by others around the cavern. The creatures bared their teeth and pounded their chests with their fists.

Lilith tightened her protective embrace around the baby, instinctively curling her body to shield it. Jacob, with a gesture of desperation, raised his hands, appealing for calm.

"Jacob," I hissed, drawing his glance. His eyes, wide with a palpable fear, mirrored the realization that dawned on both of us: he was an outsider once again. As was I.

"They're confused," he said. "They think it shoulda been born like them." He tried to reason with Warrior once more, but the beast dismissed his pleas with a sharp gesture that stirred the crowd into a roaring approval. Agitated, fearsome beasts pushed their way to the front.

A clawed hand landed heavily on Jacob's shoulder; he shrugged it off with a mix of defiance and despair. His voice was now completely lost in the swelling chaos that filled the cavern.

The mood darkened further as four imposing creatures strode forward, their eyes fixed on Warrior. One issued a throaty challenge, to which Warrior responded with a roar, standing tall. His supporters quickly rallied to his side.

Two factions were forming. A fight was brewing.

With the crowd's focus diverted, I saw my chance. Moving quietly, I edged closer to the stone slab where Jacob stood. I reached out, placing a firm hand on his arm to get his attention. *We need to leave.* He reacted swiftly, taking Lilith's hand and helping her to her feet.

I hoped we could escape before the madness descended into mayhem.

But we did not.

# CHAPTER 21

I barely recall our chaotic escape. I could hardly see, relying on Jacob and Lilith's knowledge of the Stygian tunnel systems. As we fled the main chamber, two of Warrior's allies swiftly gave chase. They were almost upon us when a group of creatures aligned with Jacob intervened, crashing into our pursuers and sending them sprawling. With our momentary reprieve, we dashed around a tight corner and disappeared into the shadowy depths of the next cavern.

The civil war among the creatures had begun. On one side, those who saw Jacob, Lilith, and the child as their hope for salvation. On the other, those furious with the notion of a human child as the tip of their racial spear. The factions clashed with the ruthlessness of a bygone era. Their death-screams could shred the nerves of any modern man.

Gasping for breath and struggling to keep pace, I followed Jacob through the winding tunnels. My legs burned, and just when I thought I might collapse from exhaustion, he slowed and veered sharply right. In the darkness, I heard the clatter of objects being hastily moved.

Suddenly, *whoosh* —

A torch flared to life.

Lilith hissed, her eyes stinging from the sudden light. Jacob passed me the torch, its warm glow a welcome relief. As my eyes adjusted, I took in our surroundings. We had entered a hidden chamber, surprisingly homely, with a mattress, a table with chairs, and a dresser.

Jacob moved with purpose, climbing up to reach an overhang in the rock. There, concealed and carefully arranged, was his cache of weapons.

He retrieved a pistol and a belt of cartridges, handing them to me. Diving back into his stash, he emerged with two more pistols and a machete. I placed the torch between some rocks to keep it upright, then set about loading the pistols, making sure each was ready. There were plenty of cartridges.

Jacob tossed me an extra pair of pants, a belt, and boots. I quickly dressed, adjusting the baggy pants as best as I could and cinching the belt tightly at its last notch. I wrapped the belt of cartridges snugly around my waist and felt a new sense of readiness with the weight of the lead secure against me.

I grabbed my gun and the torch, equipped now to face whatever lay ahead. Jacob armed himself similarly with a machete and a pistol.

Pausing as if he remembered something important, he turned back to the stash one last time. He emerged with a sack, heavy with what looked to be a dozen or so grenades. Carefully, he secured them and hung the sack over his shoulder.

Time was running short.

The screams of the hordes echoed ominously through the grottos. They would find us.

Soon.

I tugged at Jacob's arm, urging him to move.

But his mind was on other things. Deep in a heated argument with Lilith, his voice escalated. Abruptly, he handed me the baby, whom he had wrapped in a soft cloth, before turning back to continue their dispute.

A small hand emerged from the fabric and wrapped around my index finger. It was an unusual hand, with three fingers — the middle one notably larger than the others — and a thumb.

The deformity did not distract me from his face. His beautiful, normal face. Bruised, yes, so severely that his eyes remained closed. Yet already I could see the resemblance, not only to Jacob . . . but to me.

My grandson.

My nephew.

Whoever thought that from a wound so ugly could spring something so beautiful?

It *was* a miracle, wasn't it?

I held him tighter, completely lost in the boy. The tears came. I didn't stop them.

"She don't wanna go." Jacob threw his hands up, gesturing to Lilith. He looked distraught. "Can ya believe it?"

I wiped my face. "Why not?"

Jacob shook his head. "She don't trust ya."

"*Me?*"

"She scared what might happen if we take her away." He hesitated. "She right, ain't she? If she leave, go out in the world, ain't no one gonna accept her. She end up in a circus. Or dead. What happens when people find out what she is?"

Lilith turned, dropping her gaze to the child.

My son's wife, the mother of my grandson.

I stared at her. Something came over me. She recoiled as I placed my hand gently against her long face. Her scaly skin was piping hot under my touch. Her jaw trembled. But she held my gaze, and I was struck by the deep, radiant blue of her eyes, even in the dim cavern light. Compelled toward her, I stepped forward, offering a hug.

Shuddering, she returned the embrace.

And a plan crystallized in my mind.

I could secure a new home for Lilith and Jacob. Our mother's old house, I thought, could be refurbished; the baby would have the room upstairs, and Lilith could choose her own space. I could even put them in the barn, if that's where they felt most comfortable.

Yes.

I smiled. Gently handed her the child back. I then drew both her and Jacob into a close circle, my arm around my brother-son as he embraced his wife.

The thought solidified: we're a family now.

I could feel that they understood.

I stepped back slightly, my hands lingering on their shoulders. "Time to go," I said, then turned to Jacob. I made it clear that I wouldn't leave without first finding and attempting to free Bud and Private Rivers. No one would be left behind.

He glanced back at Lilith, nodded at me, and then the three of us — plus the baby — were off.

The cell was a considerable distance from the main cavern where the fighting was most intense. We hurried through the labyrinthine passages, turning this way and that, the sounds of conflict growing fainter as we delved deeper into the network of tunnels.

Finally, we stopped before a nondescript section of wall. Jacob, holding the torch aloft, nodded towards a heavy door cleverly disguised to blend with the rocky surroundings. He handed me the torch so he would be free to work. The mechanism of the lock was foreign to me, but Jacob manipulated the latches. Within moments, the door opened.

"Rivers!" I slid to the ground on my knees. The dim light fell upon him; he was slouched against the wall, a dark red stain across his belly. One hand clutched a small Bible to his chest, and his eyes were closed, his face pale and drawn.

"He's gone, sir," came a voice from the darkness.

Bud's breathing was labored, his yellow, sallow eyes flickering half-open as he lay propped against the wall, shrouded deeper in the shadows. Red gunk oozed from the corners of his mouth.

But he was alive.

"Did they . . .?" I began, my voice trailing off as I referred to Rivers.

He shook his head. "Injured . . . in the fight . . . went out . . . like a warrior . . . they never touched him . . . the good book . . . gave him strength . . . to the end." His voice was a hoarse whisper.

I moved to help him up, slipping my arms under his shoulders. A hellish pain racked his body. Grimacing, he pushed me away. "It's no use." His gaze dropped to his abdomen where his hands desperately tried to hold in his guts, spilling grotesquely between his clammy fingers.

"It's alright," he murmured, closing his eyes and leaning his head back against the cold wall. With a trembling left hand, he reached into the inner pocket of his jacket.

And emerged with the thin bottle of whiskey.

I didn't try to stop him.

He unscrewed the cap and lifted the bottle.

And poured out the brown liquid onto the stone.

The bottle slipped from his grasp, clattering on the ground.

"I did it," he said. "I'll be goin' out dry, won't I?" A smile flickered across his face.

"Yes," I said. "You will."

I stayed beside him, ignoring Jacob's anxious pleas to leave, until Bud's hand went limp. Gently, I closed his eyelids, picked up his hat, and placed it back on his head.

I stood and faced Jacob, Lilith, and their newborn. It was time. I felt a resolve firming within me.

"Let's go home —"

I heard the skittering of claws.

Suddenly, they were upon us. Jacob and Lilith cried out as two creatures crashed into them from behind. Collapsing under the assault, Lilith cradled the little one to her breast.

As I raced out of the cell to help, a third beast blindsided me, sending me smashing into the wall. My flesh tore and the bones ground as the foul-smelling ogre rammed me again and again shoulder-first into the rock. Thrown like a doll from the hands of a demented child, I hit the ground again, my right arm trapped under my own weight. Before I could react, the creature pounced, tearing flesh from my arms and back with its vicious claws. I gasped for air as its claws raked me deep — and found bone. The shock made me stiffen, back arched, while he scraped down my scapula. The fingers of God electrocuted my nerves.

Then, the crushing weight on my chest suddenly eased, and the claw tearing at my flesh withdrew. I peered back shakily.

Jacob had tackled the beast, and they were now wrestling fiercely to my right. Seizing the moment of distraction, I freed my good arm and scrambled to my feet. I drew my pistol as the creature momentarily gained the upper hand, pinning Jacob beneath it. As it reared its head back in a roar, its mouth agape —

I aimed and fired.

The brute's head snapped back, and it was swallowed by the darkness.

Silence fell over the cavern.

Stepping forward cautiously, I surveyed the scene around me. The floor was littered with bodies — three dead humanoids, each riddled with bullet holes and marked by Jacob's knife.

But —

Wait.

My heart sank.

There was another body.

Dear God.

"Lilith!" Jacob slid on his knees across the rocky floor to where she lay.

"The baby —" I looked around.

As if on cue, a cry pierced the silence. *The baby was alive.* I scooped my grandson, carefully wrapping him back in his cloth and holding him close.

Jacob curled his body protectively around his wife. Gently stroked her hair as she remained motionless. Her belly ran red and open.

His right arm appeared twisted unnaturally beneath him. As my eyes traveled down his body, I noticed a growing pool of blood. I set a hand on his back, and as he turned to look up at me, the wound in his side opened up. The puddle grew larger.

His wound was grievously deep, slicing from just under the right ribcage nearly down to his hip. Dark, almost black blood pooled around him.

They'd gotten his liver.

Setting the child down briefly, I tore off my shirt and wrapped it around Jacob's midsection, trying to stanch the bleeding.

"Too deep," he groaned. "No good."

*No.* Ignoring him, I pulled him to his feet. Standing was a miracle in itself. Once he steadied, I released him to quickly gather the baby and our belongings. We would need every gun, every bullet, every knife we could carry —

"Father."

His voice was faint. I turned to see him slumped back into the shadows, leaning half-hunched and lifeless against the wall. Beyond him, in the distance, a sliver of yellow light caught my eye.

Not firelight, though.

Daylight.

I tried to pull him from the wall. He let out an inhuman moan so pitiful and demoralized that it momentarily froze me.

"I'll . . . only slow . . . you down," he said.

Reaching down, he grasped the bundle of hand grenades. He held it tightly to his chest, his strength clearly fading, yet determined to reserve whatever remained for what he needed to do next.

"You . . . raise him. Have a family. Tell him . . . where he come from. How his father ended it. How he became something . . . from when he was nothing."

Just as he finished speaking, a screech echoed from somewhere in the tunnels. They were close. Jacob glanced into the endless dark that led deeper into the mountain. "They gotta surprise coming." He had a weak but defiant glint in his eye. "A real surprise."

With a groan, he pushed himself off the wall. His face had gone shock-white; it took all his focus and concentration to stand on his own. He paused, taking a long, affectionate look at the baby, then leaned down and gently kissed its forehead.

I handed him the torch. He would need it more than I.

The words caught in my throat. I wanted to tell him I was sorry, that I was young, that I shouldn't have left, that I didn't want to leave him now —

"Ssh," he said. "It's okay. This time . . . it's okay."

We embraced and I didn't want to let him go. Moments ago, I had been planning our future as one family. Now I would be back where I started: alone.

I suppose that's how these things go. Perhaps it had been folly to assume it could be different.

Jacob turned and staggered back into the depths of the tunnel. The first few steps were unsteady and cautious, but gradually, he found his footing. The torchlight bobbed in the darkness, casting fleeting shadows until it disappeared altogether.

As if sensing his father's departure, the baby in my arms began to cry.

I held it closer, whispering a soft goodbye to Jacob in my heart.

Then, with the child secure, I turned toward the sunrise, and ran.


I didn't stop running, not even after we emerged from the tunnels on the other side of the mountain. The ground trembled beneath me, and a muffled, warlike explosion echoed from within the rock. Glancing back in the dim light of dawn, I witnessed the mountain collapse upon itself — trees toppled, and the earth caved in above the tunnel, swallowing any trace of pursuit.


Fortune smiled upon us then, and good luck continued for the rest of our journey. The first night was mild, requiring only a modest fire. At dawn, I managed to shoot a deer, and although the child was too young for the meat, I carefully squeezed a bit of blood into his mouth. It seemed to suffice.

Even more fortunate was the trail on this side of the mountain. We made quick progress, descending swiftly and covering about twenty miles without difficulty each day. After three days, we encountered a small community of homesteaders nestled in a canyon between two rugged hills flanking a river. They gave us aid and tended to my wounds. Remarkably, one of the daughters, having recently given birth, was able to nurse the child.

Two weeks later, we returned to Ironwood, traveling in a covered wagon. As I stepped out into the bright sunshine, the boy in my arms, there was Angie sweeping the front porch of Headhunter's. I took her hand gently and told her it was time to pack her things. This would be her last shift as a barmaid.

For we were going to be rich.

The humanoids may have been decimated and the hills shattered, yet the gold remained. Time cannot diminish it, nor can the fiercest heat obliterate it. Gold is eternal. In a world of constant change, it is the one unchanging thing. In its world, there is no evolution, no missing links, no sudden leaps forward. That is its power.

It's why men have killed each other for it, gone to war to obtain it. It's impossible to produce; it can only be discovered, claimed, smelted, sold. Try to destroy it. You cannot. It can only be reclaimed, exchanged by someone else. Human values may change. But it does not.

It is always fought for.

Sometimes you win.

# EPILOGUE

Hunter Canon exhales a tired breath as he bids goodnight to his wife and two children, then steps into the crisp evening air. His neighbors, Edwin and Martin Loftus, father and son, are already waiting down the road. Each is equipped for the night ahead with a rifle and a pistol, along with canteens and dried meat.

After two weeks of performing the nightly rounds, their routine has become second nature. Similar patrols are underway on the west and north sides of town, each team moving with the same intent and equipment. All carry torches, but not to scare the enemy.

The light just makes them feel safer.

As they reach the outskirts of Ironwood, Canon takes a deliberate turn to the right, heading towards the town's boundary. Approaching the guards stationed there, who are standing firm and dressed in tricorn hats, he pauses briefly. Recognizing him, they nod and pull open the large wrought iron gate, allowing Canon and the Loftuses to pass into the night beyond.

Once inside the compound, he stays to the right, circles the main house, and approaches the two-story brick home around back. He sees light from the candles inside, I'm sure, because that's how I want it.

He walks up to my porch and knocks.

"Making our sweep tonight," Canon announces as I open the door. "Wanted to see how you're holding up."

I shrug and wipe my greasy hands on a towel. "Doing fine." My gaze drifts to the rifle slung over August's shoulder. "More sheep gone missing?"

He nods solemnly. "Most every night. But something else has come up. That's why I wanted to stop in." He sighs and removes his hat. "We've got word that *men* are missing, too. On the south side. Two this week. They just up and vanished." His voice tightens. "I think they were taken."

I ask if they've found any clues, anything that could help them track the culprit.

"Maybe. We heard a rumor. About a sighting," he replies cautiously.

"Oh?"

"Young boy, you know James Powell's son?"

"Eight or nine years old?"

"Right. Claims he saw something. A man or . . . something resembling a man, crouched low in the field, running fast. Ungodly fast. Through the corn fields behind his house."

"And?" I sense there's more he's hesitant to say.

"Whatever it was out there, the boy hasn't spoken since. He's not even of age, and two days ago his hair turned white as snow. No explanation."

Silence hangs between us.

He continues. "Anyway, word is you had some experience with something like this before. Years back, at a mine somewhere. That right?" He pauses, scrutinizing me. "Or maybe that was just a rumor."

Suddenly, I feel very old. I sense the folds in my skin, the drooping bags around my eyes. The slight stoop in my shoulders.

*Years back, yes, at a mine somewhere.*

I shake my head slowly, meeting his gaze squarely. "Nope. Not me. You know how rumors start."

Canon nods, seemingly satisfied. "You be careful tonight. And if you do see or hear anything out of the ordinary, you'll let me know?"

"Of course."

Canon turns and heads back through the gate, toward the road where his compatriots wait. I watch until he disappears from view, the tricorn-hatted guards shutting and locking the gate behind him.

I wish them well tonight. It's dangerous out there.

Inside, I set the table for our dinner of chicken with garlic and onions. I set two places — for me and Angie — while she quietly sets a third. From behind the counter she removes a plate of lamb loins and various organs, prepared just the way the boy likes them. I snatch a piece of bread for myself, cross the room, and draw the heavy shutters closed.

Privacy is best these days.

I call out once for the boy, then again, and after the old wooden attic door creaks and groans open, I hear the familiar thud of heavy legs making their way down.

When he sits, we bow our heads for a quick prayer.

His claws have grown so much. He no longer needs utensils; his nails, sharp and precise, carve and scrape meat off the bone as efficiently as any knife. He works skillfully on the raw meat.

I note the sounds of raspy inhalation as he devours the flesh. The air down here, off the mountain, has never been good for his allergies. I frown. His nose, clogged with a familiar green pus, makes for bad manners.

"Patrols are out again tonight," I mention to Angie as we eat in the dim light of the kitchen. "Best to have Jacob Jr. stay in."

"Can't he work in the barn?" Angie asks, mindful of disappointing him.

"I don't think it's a good idea. Too many eyes on us right now."

Struggling to breathe, Jacob lets out a low, moaning sound.

"I know you're upset," I tell him. "All these nights cooped up in the attic. But they can't be helped."

His head droops. Mopey, just like any fourteen-year-old would be.

Still, it makes me reconsider. I know he's been uncomfortable lately. All he has to look forward to are his nightly mating attempts, and even those have been fewer and farther between lately.

"I suppose . . ." I pause. "You can work in the barn tonight."

He perks up, making sounds of delight.

"But only if you finish your dinner," I add firmly, turning back to Angie. "And I'll need to confirm with Price."

Jacob Jr. doesn't need to be told twice. He dives face-first into his lamb organs.

"Why does Price need to keep tabs on our comings and goings?" Angie frowns. "It's none of his business."

"It's *all* our business. We're partners, and he helps protect us, you know that." I glance at Junior. "All of us."

I watch him eat. Lately I've marveled at how fast puberty has altered his features.

His nose has become long and wide like the snout of his mother. His second set of teeth is mostly fanged and nearly double in size. Today, they jut out of his head at all angles, except for his eyeteeth, which stab straight down in points. He has no hair on the top of his head; his flesh is smooth like a humanoid's. One eye is permanently cast downward, though his vision seems unaffected. His ears retain a humanlike appearance, but his feet mirror the peculiar prints we discovered in the sand those years ago. He communicates in hisses, squeals, and grunts; despite years of effort to teach him English, it's become clear that his vocal cords are simply not suited for human speech.

Once he turned thirteen, we began the mating rituals. It was time to make an attempt. Although we haven't succeeded with the few men we've captured, time is on our side.

I suck the chicken grease from my fingers.

The work of building anew will resume tonight, I decide. While he strives to conceive, I will continue my work on the bible for the new race. The stories of a boy born under the most extraordinary circumstances, a boy destined to save the lineage of the humanoids.

The human race will no longer be the only sentient bipedal mammals.

Price and I are determined to see this through.

Around us, society is transforming. A man named Edison has just invented the incandescent light bulb, which will make candles obsolete. Something called a telephone promises instant communication across vast distances. Oil is poised to become the fuel of the future.

Yes, a new world is emerging from the old.

And our family will be the tip of the spear. Slow evolution, it turns out, is not the whole truth. Nature does not develop and transform slowly — rather, it lurches forward in gigantic, nonlinear steps.

That's why there is no missing link for us humans.

It does not exist.

For eighteen years I ran away from the terrible secret of my life, the unspeakable thing created by the sins of my mother. I've been to war and back, killed many men, and yet nothing could stem the shame. As I've learned, everything unfolds in God's time. In my glasses I wear new lenses, for what happened to me has been turned into something grand and meaningful. I have created life, and survived long enough to see *it* survive. I weep now, not out of shame, but out of love for this world and everything in it.

I wait for my grandson-nephew to finish his meal. I'm filled with gratitude for the blessings of this new era.

Nature works best when it's tamed by man, Price once said.

I have come to agree with him.

For this boy is not merely human nor beast.

He is change.

He is the future.

He's strange.

Different.

Unnamable.

# ACKNOWLEDGEMENTS

This book was inspired by H.P. Lovecraft's story "The Unnamable." It started out as a public domain continuation of his work, but as the story shifted, it no longer fit in his universe. I've left a couple homages to that original story, and some nods to those in his writing circle.

Many thanks to those who read early drafts of the screenplay that later became this book. These include Stephen Chrabaszcz, Chris Glatis, and Sebastian Ruan. Also thank you to Abby Cooper-Gayman for her notes on the manuscript, Karen Conlin for her editing, and Jordan Harris, Rickey Mizuno, Brad Geis, John Dwyer, and Hannah Nance for their various work on the cover.

Of course, thank you to Jack Ketchum, Robert McCammon, Shirley Jackson, and Robert E. Howard.

# ABOUT THE AUTHOR

Andrew Schrader is a Los Angeles-based author and filmmaker. In addition to directing feature films and music videos, he wrote several episodes of the animated show *Tig n' Seek* for Cartoon Network. He was also a script consultant on "Afterlife," the horror series from Crypt TV.

His three-book series, *What Goes On In The Walls at Night*, was featured on the Reddit No Sleep podcast and twice won the Red City Review Book of the Year for fantasy and horror. His book, *Bad Realities*, received an Editor's Recommendation from Kirkus Reviews.

Yes, of course he loves cats.

Read more at:
www.andrewjschrader.com